The author's first book was published in 2016. Swapna has lived in the UK for a long period of time. She is a mother of two adult children and enjoys travelling, walking and writing. Her favourite TV show is *Only Fools and Horses* (1981–2003). Swapna's passion for writing started approximately six years ago, mainly pleasure writing. However, she decided to publish a collection of short stories and was successful in finding a publisher who supported her dream.

The author is career-orientated and works in local government – a job she thoroughly enjoys. Swapna also keenly follows national and global affairs, and environmental issues and animal welfare are important causes to her. Contributing to the community through philanthropic activities gives the author a great satisfaction and fulfilment.

## A Verse for Cecil

The summer nightfall came soon;
The air was still and the land in full bloom.
The full white moon smiled down at Earth
As Cecil lay lazily on the carpeted grassland
He looked sideways and admired his snoozing pride
His golden mane shining in the moonlit light.
Cecil heaved a heavy sigh
As the large bee flew away from his eye.
The king of the jungle was ready to sleep.
He yawned and stretched his wide mouth and thought deep
But for the scent of carcass,
Cecil could not fall asleep
He silently followed the smelly trail
And dared to cross the forbidden lane
For their lay the trap of the savage human kind!

****

Swapna Das

# THE FORGOTTEN PEOPLE

To

Spellow Library.

from

Swapna Das
5/8/24

AUSTIN MACAULEY PUBLISHERS™

LONDON • CAMBRIDGE • NEW YORK • SHARJAH

A CIP catalogue record for this title is available from the British Library.

ISBN 9781528919043 (Paperback)
ISBN 9781528919050 (Hardback)
ISBN 9781528962544 (ePub e-book)

www.austinmacauley.com

First Published (2019)
Austin Macauley Publishers Ltd
25 Canada Square
Canary Wharf
London
E14 5LQ

Thank you to all the well-wishers who have encouraged me to write and share my stories.

# Chapter 1
## Journey to the Unknown

Panchkuri, a small tribal village stood pompously on the banks of the River Maheshwari in eastern India. It boasted of a small population of hardworking and proud people whose generations have lived there for many centuries. The land was blessed with lush green foliage and wildlife which was the envy of the neighbour states. The nearest metropolis of Kaliput was three hours' drive. The tribal people were well known for holding on to their age-old traditions of family and social values. Their respect for nature and wildlife had earned them a good reputation, as they believed that nature had to be preserved and revered. The village was unspoilt by modern life and technology, and its emerald landscape was a far cry from the concrete one a few hundred miles away.

The late night train had just pulled up at the small station and the platform was conspicuous by the absence of vendors and the din of a busy day. Rahul Bagchi, a newly qualified man of medicine, slowly stepped down from the four-bogie train holding one large suitcase in his hand and a sling bag across his shoulder. He looked somewhat confused as this was his first journey to a remote part of India, late at night. He asked a fellow passenger where he could find transport, but the man politely avoided the question and went about his business. Rahul stood for a few minutes for the crowd to disappear. From a distance, he noticed the night guard and decided to ask for help from him. As he approached the uniformed man, Rahul began to panic, for he remembered being told by his father that language barrier was a common problem for visitors. Determined to succeed, Rahul courteously introduced himself and asked the man to help him to find conveyance. The conversation that followed between the two men brought a smile on Rahul's anxious face, for luckily, the night guard, who introduced himself as Soren, was able to understand the new visitor. After a short journey, the rickshaw stopped at the front of a bungalow just on the outskirts of Panchkuri. Rahul was greeted by two elderly men. The rickshaw driver was paid handsomely by his passenger, and with a delighted look on his face, he drove away slowly towards the other side of the road.

The rumbling of the night sky kept Rahul awake for most of the night as he lay in his rocking four-poster bed. He stared at the ceiling and remembered his family and friends he had left behind in Kaliput. Although he was delighted to be offered the job of a district doctor by the government. Initially, he was apprehensive about travelling to the unfamiliar location of Panchkuri. Rahul took up the challenge of serving in the remote village and assured his family that he would look after himself and keep in contact with them with regular phone calls. On his first night at Panchkuri, Rahul discovered that the village was not served with telephone connection. "Life is not going to be easy," Rahul said aloud and left his bed to drink some water. He avoided dinner as he was not hungry, having eaten in the train. The monsoon rain pounded down on the land, and the young doctor could hear it hit against the windows, the room felt cooler and sleep was nowhere in his mind. Fortunately, Rahul did not have to report for work the next day, so he had the luxury to stay up late and settle in his bedroom and tidy his belongings. He unpacked his suitcase and took out the small pocket transistor his brother had gifted him as a farewell present. He tried to tune in to the local radio station, and then he reminded himself that the village may not have a radio station. He tried desperately to tune into another station but was not successful, as frustration slowly crept in, Rahul momentarily thought he may have made a wrong career decision. "Luxury is not going to be part of my life here," Rahul grumbled to himself as he finally fell asleep in his new home.

Rahul was awakened early next morning by a loud knock on his front door, half-asleep, he heard voices outside. He hurriedly stood up and wore his shirt; he looked outside from his window and saw five men and two elderly women talking in an unknown language. Uncertain as to who the visitors were, the young man gathered courage and greeted the group. The villagers were talking in their dialect, but Rahul could not understand a word, then one of the women pointed to the basket of food and gestured to her friend. The six men and the women communicated, but they understood very little what Rahul had to say; therefore, the conversation was not making headway. Fortunately, Rahul recognised a familiar face approaching the house; he immediately recognised Soren, the night guard. The man approached the group and spoke to Rahul, "They have come to clean your house and cook your food." He looked at the basket of fruit and vegetable and courteously instructed the women to go inside the house. The matter settled, the group of men dispersed and Soren advised Rahul that he lived nearby and wrote down his address on a piece of white paper in case Rahul needed help. "Learn the language quickly, sir, if you wish to integrate in the small community." Soren departed with a friendly smile on his face. Rahul could hear the women chatting inside the house as they went about their chores, and the smell of food increased his appetite and Rahul looked forward to his breakfast.

It had stopped raining the next day, and the bright sun awakened Rahul early. The smell of the rain was fresh, and Rahul admired the morning beauty whilst looking out of his window. After a short while, he readied himself and decided to explore the village on his own. Before leaving, he drank a cup of tea and a toast as he noticed the women approach the house. The three of them greeted each other with folded hands and a broad smile. The two tall women introduced each other as Gauri and Sonamuni. Rahul was pleased that slowly the language barrier would break, and he promised himself to make an earnest effort to learn the local dialect. He pointed to the outside of the house and gestured to the two ladies that he was going for a walk in the village. With an endearing smile on their face, Gauri and Sonamuni nodded their head and pointed to the umbrella for Rahul to take – he remembered that it was the monsoon season and rain could be expected any time. The doctor left his home feeling more relaxed as he gently walked on the winding pebbled road which headed towards Panchkuri.

The air felt fresh and the early morning sun was bright, and as he walked, the newly arrived doctor slowly observed the backdrop of the village. On the journey, he was greeted by the local people, some of them with a curious look on their face, whilst others preferred to stop and greet him. By the second day, the villagers had come to know that a new district doctor had arrived and seeing the new face, they assumed that he was the doctor. Rahul noticed children playing in the field, and men attending to the rice fields that stretched on both sides of the road. Rahul had never seen such beauty, the green landscape was spotted with mango, guava, jackfruit, bedana, bamboo and palm trees. Only a few women could be seen fetching water from the pond as they gracefully walked holding the earthen pot on the slim waist. Rahul was also surprised to see a smile on everyone, adults and children, and this cheered him up. Suddenly, he was stopped by a herd of cows crossing the road, and a man introduced himself as Akash, and to the young doctor's surprise, he spoke fluently in Bengali, and Akash could see the relief on Rahul's face. "Finally, I have found a person who understands my mother tongue. Thank you, Panchkuri," Rahul uttered in a hurry. The two men laughed together and became instant friends and they walked the remaining journey together, chatting and laughing all the way.

\*\*\*\*

# Chapter 2
## Home Away from Home

As Rahul became familiar with his surroundings, home and the natives of Panchkuri; he was confident that life would be comfortable in his new place. However, occasionally, his thoughts would drift towards Kaliput and his family. The absence of electricity and modern amenities in the village made him feel homesick. However, for the young doctor, friendships were not hard to make as the village language had become easier to pick up and understand. Santra Medical Centre was a busy place, and women and children would visit in hundreds during a good week. The job kept Rahul busy throughout the day, and apart from his regular job as the district doctor, he often made unplanned home visits to families who could not make the journey to the centre. Soon, his kindness and commitment to his patients became known which earned him the respect of everyone, including the leader of the *panchayat*.

Rahul's three-bedroom cosy bungalow was well decorated and maintained by Gauri and Sonamuni, who would promptly arrive in the morning to prepare the breakfast and clean the house. As the doctor had learned a few local words, he would join in the conversation, and they would often laugh and joke together. Waving his hand, Rahul would often greet the ladies as he hurriedly left the house. On the way, he would pick up some fruits from a local vendor and walk to the medical centre.

On the first day of work, Rahul was pleased to discover that the medical centre had electricity, and he noticed a squeaky ceiling fan and a light in the two large main examination rooms. On reaching his workplace, almost as a ritual, Rahul would wash his hands before he attended to his patients. His assistant, Ramlal, would help to set up everything in the large adjoining room. The medical centre was inaugurated two years ago by the local minister; however, infrastructure in the village was much to be desired. Painstakingly, Rahul would treat the people with limited resources, and his medical knowledge and skill was highly appreciated by most of the natives. The only exception being an elderly group of men and women who did not share the same interest in modern medicine and chose to rely on the services of a well-known local medicine man. The group of men and women would often taunt the city doctor as he tended to his people, but their behaviour did not have an impact on Rahul as he was determined to make a success of his career in the small village.

One day, Ramlal came running to the room and he spoke hurriedly, "Come quickly, doctor, the child is not breathing." Rahul quickly stepped outside and saw a boy in his father's arms lying still with his eyes closed.

The father was weeping as he addressed Rahul – "Please save my son, Doctor *babu*, I don't know what has happened, he was playing outside." The man stopped for a brief period, then spoke again, "I heard him scream, and I ran outside to find my son lying still on the floor; he was not breathing." Having listened to the details, Rahul quickly examined the boy, and having realised that there was very little time, Rahul instructed Ramlal to get his medical case from the room. He opened the briefcase and took out a syringe and a small medicine bottle, he then proceeded to give the boy an injection and waited anxiously to see the result. There was silence in the room and the group of men and women waited patiently for a miracle to happen. Rahul pressed his lips but did not display any signs of doubt, for he was confident that the medicine he had administered would work effectively, and it did. Within a few minutes, the small boy started to move his fingers and his toes. Everyone breathed a sigh of relief, and the boy's father repeatedly thanked the young doctor and fondly called him *jadugar* (magician). He listened to all the instructions the doctor repeated, and the crowd then left the medical centre discussing about the district doctor's medical skills.

As a token of gratitude, the next day the boy's father presented Rahul with a basket of fresh vegetables and fruits. At first, the doctor refused to accept the gift, but the grateful man was persistent, and, finally, Rahul received the gift with gratitude.

As Rahul ate his dinner that night, he recalled the events of the day and thought deeply about his medical profession, and reminded himself that it was also a vocation. He was grateful that he had the opportunity to save a life within the short time he had taken up the post. He felt a flow of immense satisfaction and the motivation to work in the community and serve its people; he also felt connected to his adopted village. Whilst in deep thought, he suddenly realised that he had not written a letter to his parents about his arrival at the place, "My parents must be thinking about me," Rahul said aloud, "I must write a letter to them today." He settled himself on the chair next to the window and placed the writing pad on the table. Rahul began to write his first letter from Panchkuri:

*Pranam, Ma and Baba, sorry that I did not write earlier, life got busy in the village. I have settled well in Panchkuri. It is a beautiful land of friendly and proud people. The community has welcomed me with their open arms, and I have picked up a few local words which has helped me to make friends easily. Gauri and Sonamuni take care of the home, and they cook me delicious food; however, I still miss ma's food.*

*My first test as the district doctor happened today, and because of quick thinking, I was able to save a child's life. I was anxious at first, but my faith in my profession surpassed my fear; the natives were grateful and as a token of their love, I was presented with a basket full of fresh fruits and vegetable which I gladly accepted. It will be served on my dinner table for the next few days.*

*The village huts are beautifully decorated outside and there is a tree outside. Most of the villagers own cattle. The cows look very healthy and produce sufficient milk and cater for the whole village. Panchkuri is a small village of approximately 1000 inhabitants. Its people are proud of their heritage and takes offence to any criticism of their lifestyle, so I am careful not to say anything and nod my head in appreciation wherever I go.*

*Surprisingly, the medical centre where I work has electricity, and there are plans for the entire village to be electrified soon and phone connections will follow. I will let you know when this happens.*

*Don't be concerned for me. I am fine, and hope you are also keeping well. I promise I will write frequently to keep you updated about my life in a remote part of the country and my 'home away from home'.*

*With lots love to you,*
*Rahul.*

\*\*\*\*

# Chapter 3
## The Medicine Man

The following weeks of the monsoon season were busy for the young doctor in Panchkuri. Rahul's day would start early and finish late as he treated people of all ages. In particular, children were his common patients. The riverbanks had swollen due to the persistent downpour and villagers became increasingly anxious about a possible deluge. The rugged huts could not withstand the violent showers, and people would try to adapt and protect their homes and family. Different skin diseases were spreading within the small population, and Rahul was struggling to keep up with the demands of his patients. On occasions, medicine was out of stock, and regular fresh orders had to be placed with the main store in the city; however, due to the water-logged roads, it was hard for the additional stock to be delivered on time. Several weeks passed by, and the chaos of rainy season continued, and during such difficult moments, Rahul would feel frustrated and helpless, as he remembered and yearned for his comfortable life in the city.

For a few days, Rahul had noticed the medical centre was less busy than usual, despite the outbreak of diseases, people would pass by and greet him with a nod. Rahul did not think much about it, for he thought that the ailment must have been contained naturally. A few blocks away from the medical centre, there was a cluster of eleven thatched huts built by the local people. Rahul had noticed these isolated huts but did not think too much about it, neither did he meet any of its residents. On certain days, from his window, he could see groups of people heading towards the location of the huts, women carrying their children, and one particular green coloured hut attracted most of the villagers. With time, Rahul's curiosity was stirred, but he avoided asking anyone about the sudden flurry of activity in the nearby block. He kept a watchful eye on the coming and goings of the villagers from that direction. The green hut was the main focus of the doctor's curious attention. As his home visits were less due to sudden outbursts of the cloud, most of the time Rahul stayed indoors. Often, some elderly men would come and sit outside on the veranda and engage in casual conversation with their doctor.

One day, Rahul took the courage and innocently asked the three men seated outside about the green hut in the nearby block. Rahul informed them that he had noticed the hut being frequented by his known patients. The three bearded men scratched their head and looked at one another, each expecting the other person to reply to him. After a brief silence, one of the men informed Rahul that a local medicine man lived in the green hut for many years; his knowledge and skill about ayurvedic medicine was well known, and he had treated different types of ailments for a number of years. The man continued to speak, and said, "During the rainy season, people thronged his home to get medicine, and they were never disappointed by the result."

"What is his name, and is he a qualified doctor?" Rahul hurriedly asked. The men again looked at each other, not knowing what to say, but they all said in a chorus that the villagers had accepted the medicine man as their saviour during the wet season and during times of crisis. Rahul had a confused look on his face as he stared at the three senior men, he quickly added, "What is his name, and why does the medicine man treat only during the rainy season?" Rahul's curiosity and interest about the mysterious medicine man had increased.

"His name is Mathal," one of the men replied hurriedly, and then the three men quickly stood up and departed from Rahul's company. The doctor stood still and watched the men leave without answering all the questions.

That evening, Rahul took the suspense home, and as he walked, his mind was preoccupied with thoughts about his local competitor.

The weekend arrived slowly, but for Rahul, it was long awaited because he made plans to make more enquiries about the 'medicine man'. He woke up early on Sunday and welcomed the women who had arrived to do the household chores, and after an appetising breakfast, Rahul left the home in pursuit of knowledge about the man the villagers called their saviour. Soon, he was joined by the night guard. "Good morning, Soren. Where are you going?" Rahul casually asked. Soren replied saying he was going to see the medicine man, as he needed medicine for his ailing wife. Rahul had a surprised look on his face as he discovered that even his new friend relied on Mathal during the rainy season. He was tempted to offer his companion conventional medicine, but Rahul refrained, as he had doubts that his offer of help may be snubbed. The two men walked in silence for the remainder of their journey.

As they arrived at the hut, Rahul had noticed a long queue of villagers outside waiting anxiously to be seen by their saviour. Small children held on to their parents' hand, whilst a few children slept in their mothers' arms. Rahul could hear whispers amongst the crowd that had gathered outside the hut as Rahul heard a gentle male voice from inside speak to his patient. Rahul managed to peep through the half-open grilled window facing the east side. He noticed an elderly man with a long, grey beard and hair seated on the bed, examining a child's body. He then gently tapped the child's belly with the index finger and raised the child's head. Rahul was very fascinated by what he was witnessing, and he made sure that no other person stood near the window to block his view. He positioned himself strategically to prevent this from happening. He again leaned against the window and continued to observe everything that was going on inside the room. In the meantime, Mathal had placed the child on his folded lap, poured some liquid from a small container and gave it to the sick child to drink. Then he spoke with a dignified voice and told the mother, "Bring your child again tomorrow at the same time, give him a good bath with warm water and put him to sleep early." Having listened to the instructions from the man, the mother paid her respect, bowed her head and carried her child outside. She looked relaxed and hurriedly left the hut. The child was the eighth patient the man had seen within an hour; Rahul was told by another onlooker. As he watched the unfolding scenes, Rahul was intrigued as well as confused, but he said nothing to anyone and walked back home. On his return journey, he asked himself, *Only during the wet season Mathal practices his skill… Why?*

Rahul was confident that he would know the answer sooner or later, it was a matter of time before everything became clear. As soon as he reached his home, there was a cloudburst as if the rain god has spewed his wrath on the lush green land, and Rahul wisely decided to stay indoors for the rest of the day. He drank his favourite brew and began to read the medical journal that had been delivered the day before. He suddenly remembered from a brief conversation with the postman in the morning that there was a beautiful forest nearby, beyond the adjoining hills, that boasted of a spectacular sunrise. Rahul had promised the postman that one day he would visit the nature spot and enjoy the morning glory.

****

# Chapter 4
## Shorai *Mela* (Fair)

After three months of prolonged rainfall and disarray, the little hamlet of Panchkuri was slowly returning to normalcy, apart from the outbreak of a mysterious illness. On their part, the Department of Health was putting its best effort to contain the spread of the disease, and Rahul was responsible for its management in the village. Mathal was busy too, for there was always a queue outside his house, and on one day, Rahul had commented to a passer-by, "The man is making more money than me."

"He does not take any money from his patients," prompt came the reply from the man.

Due to the deluge, the rice fields were flooded; therefore, the farmers were seriously affected, and it impacted on their income and economy in general as Panchkuri produced the most sought-after fragranced rice grain in the country. However, for the nature lovers, the land was in its full coloration, the bright green leaves looked washed, the rare monsoon flowers, white, pink and lilac adorned the landscape and the seasonal fruit was much in demand. For the young doctor, it was an overwhelming experience. Despite his hectic life, he rarely missed the morning sunrise breaking through the dark clouds, the early morning cawing of a crow, and if Rahul was lucky, he would see a monkey busily picking on the fruits of the nearby trees; however, on occasions, he felt intimidated by the presence of the monkeys, even though they were busy causing havoc in the tress rather than to a human.

The River Maheshwari was full to its brim, but it was not a precarious situation for the village, and within a few weeks, the water level had subsided. On the rare occasions, when Rahul finished work early, he would stop by the river and look at the *nouko* (country boat) and would promise himself that he must find time for a boat ride, and one day, he asked one of the boatmen, "How long does it take to cross the river?"

The boatman looked surprised and said, "This is not the right time to take a boat ride, Doctor *babu*, let the river settle; it usually takes an hour to cross the river depending on the tide." Rahul greeted the man and parted his company. As he continued his journey back home, he noticed a man lying outside a hut in an unconscious state, his pet dog whimpered nearby and watched over his master. Rahul had an uncanny feeling that something was wrong, so he approached the body, he then looked around to see if there was anyone else in the hut.

"Is anyone at home," Rahul called out aloud, there was an eerie silence. The doctor then looked at the man, raised his limp hand and checked his pulse, and was relieved to feel the pulse beats. Fortunately, the downpour had stopped, and Rahul managed to draw the attention of some passers-by. The group of three men at once recognised the district doctor and was eager to help him. "We need to carry the man inside the hut," Rahul politely instructed the men. The sick man's body was placed on an old bed; the absence of bedding was noticed by Rahul.

The three villagers looked at each other and at the ill man and questioned Rahul, "Is he alive, Doctor *babu*?" Rahul nodded his head and proceeded to examine the man. Having waited for more than thirty minutes and with no signs of movement from the sick man, despite the medication, Rahul began to be concerned.

The group of four men waited patiently for the situation to improve, but it was not to be, as Rahul realised that the patient would need a timely hospital admission, and the doctor's suspicion about the man's illness increased with every minute. He again addressed the men slowly, "He has to be admitted to a hospital, are you able to arrange transport?"

"Yes," the men replied in a chorus. By late afternoon, the man was transported to a nearby large government hospital. Rahul had written an urgent letter addressed to the emergency doctor and requested for an early treatment for the man. After three days, as Rahul walked to his medical centre, he noticed the man he had saved approaching him, Tamun introduced himself to the doctor and said, "Thank you, doctor, you saved my life. You are kind."

Rahul smiled and replied, "I only helped to send you to the hospital; you were saved by the hospital doctors and staff, you must thank them." Tamun promised to express his gratitude soon.

Following a few months, the district doctor had made a good impression in the village and people would show their respect to him, whenever the opportunity came. In the meantime, Mathal's contribution to his people did not go unnoticed by Rahul, for he, too, was playing his role by treating sick men, women and children, without a price tag. Slowly and steadily, the village was the hometown of two reputed doctors, albeit they pursued different methods of treatment and practice. But to Tamun, the district doctor was his saviour, even though he had deep respect for non-traditional medicine. With the passage of time, the city doctor became Tamun's confidante, and he was privy to Tamun's innermost thoughts. Rahul came to know that Tamun had tragically lost his young wife during the worst floods in recent times; he became unemployed soon and had been living a poor standard of life. Rahul empathised with his new friend, and often offered valuable advice, which Tamun took on board. One day, Tamun said to the doctor, "The Shorai *Mela* (fair) will start in a few weeks, and the cattle market is also held at the same time." Rahul looked at Tamun and told him that he had heard about the annual event. The two men then agreed to visit the *mela*; therefore, on the day of the fair, Tamun opened his late wife's small pink purse, which he had treasured in a dainty wooden box, and took out a gold necklace. He looked at the choker and felt the tear drops on his cheeks. Tamun then, hesitantly, placed the item in his crumpled white *kurta* (tunic) pocket and left the hut.

It was a sunny and warm day, and people had thronged the Shorai *Mela*. Most visitors wore bright coloured clothes. Children were busy buying candy and coloured balloons. The funfair boasted of exciting rides, there were different stalls selling local handicrafts, and the food stalls appeared to be the most popular ones. Vendors did brisk business, and the ambience was one of gaiety and merriment. One man stood with a large metal box, as he addressed the crowd in his baritone voice, "Come and see coloured photos and pictures, this is a magic box." As he pointed to his kaleidoscope, Tamun watched the children run towards him with enthusiasm and stood patiently to see inside the mysterious tin box. He was soon joined by the doctor who had finished treating his last patient on the Sunday at his home. Rahul was keen to visit the market, as he had promised Tamun. The adjacent cattle market was crowded with buyers and sellers, and Tamun watched the proceedings from a distance. His main reason to attend the cattle market was to purchase a healthy calf or a cow, if possible, in exchange for the gold necklace. The bidding for the paraded animals began with fervour and prospective buyers offered their price for the most sought after cattle. The prices they offered were beyond Tamun's ability, and for a brief moment, he looked on helplessly as he saw the healthy cattle disappear from the market. Only eleven cows had remained unsold, but Tamun could not afford the healthy ones; therefore, his attention was drawn towards an emaciated black and white spotted cow which he knew was unlikely to be bid for. Taking advantage of the situation and after a brief conversation with its owner, Tamun purchased the cow and left the market, holding his new companion by the rope around her thin neck.

On the way back home, the new owner stopped and looked at the cow's wide black eyes, patted her back and in a friendly voice said, "You will make me rich and happy." He had not noticed that the doctor was not far behind him and had heard what Tamun had said to the cow. Although the doctor had a smile on his face, he was surprised to hear the comment, but could not guess the reason for it.

****

# Chapter 5
## Nandini

The day at the fair was long and tiring. Tamun and his new friend arrived home early evening. The cow followed her master obediently and sat at the entrance of the hut. Tamun gave her some water and spoke to her. "I like the name Nandini; therefore, I will call you by that name." The cow slowly nodded her head and looked sideways to the grass patch, and as she was hungry, she stood up and walked to the green spot and began to chew the grass. Tamun was hungry too, so he washed his hand and went inside. There was very little food inside, except for the *muri* (puffed rice) in a bowl. Tamun had no money for milk, so he decided to have the morsel of food with a glass of water. After finishing his food, Tamun came outside again and looked at the skinny animal sat on the front porch. Tamun already felt a bond for the animal, and promised to take good care of her. For a brief moment, both the white cow and Tamun exchanged a look of belonging and closeness. He picked up a large torn jute sack and placed it on the cow's back. "I will do the ritual tomorrow morning; in the meantime, you try and have a good night sleep," Tamun addressed the cow. 'Moo' came the quick reply.

The long established social and religious tradition of the native tribe was followed passionately, and for Tamun, the practice held a very important role in his life. The bow and arrow was a vital part of Panchkuri's social and recreational life. Apart from hunting, the weapon was also used for religious purpose. When Tamun was a teenager, he was gifted with a decorated longbow and arrow by his father, and he had treasured the gift. He used it on special occasion, so the next day, Tamun took out the bow and arrow from under the bed. He removed the dust and looked at it admiringly, as he remembered his father. At dawn, Tamun had heard the cow call out, and it was a reminder from his new companion to tend to her. After a shower, Tamun went outside and called out to Nandini. She recognised her name and looked at her cheerful master holding a bow and arrow. Tamun then bathed the animal with a good scrub. This was followed by a ceremonial procedure – he looked up to the blue sky, addressed his forefathers, lifted the longbow in his hands and prayed to the gods for the safety and welfare of the animal. He then gently placed the bow on the cow's forehead and smiled at her showing his sparkling white teeth. Nandini graciously accepted the blessings of the gods and her master, and mooed again reminding her master that it was time for breakfast.

With limited money in his possession, Tamun realised that he had to maintain, not just himself but Nandini also. He had grand plans for Nandini; he would do everything possible to make a livelihood as a *gwala* (milkman). But first, he focused his attention to find food for the cow, so he went out to the nearby green field holding a sickle in his hand and a big sack. With speed and precision, Tamun cut the long grass and within an hour, he had collected enough fodder for the animal. He returned home with a full sack of grass and gave half of it to the cow. She was pleased with her first meal of the day. "You have bought a cow from the cattle market, Tamun," asked Santra, as the owner was suddenly interrupted.

Santra was Tamun's long-time friend, and he replied, "Yes, it was not easy, and I had to bargain with the owner." Santra observed the cow and commented that she was very thin and may not live long, he also added that the cow was neglected by her previous master.

"I will make her strong and healthy," Tamun promised to the friend. The two men then went inside the hut for a friendly chat leaving the animal to enjoy her food.

Tamun and Santra discussed about various subjects, including Tamun's dream to be a successful *gwala*. He was confident that Nandini would produce milk soon, and he would be able to sell the milk in the local market. Santra encouraged him to speak to the *panchayat* head to seek permission to gather grass from the fields to provide fodder for Nandini. Tamun said, "Yes it is important that I have regular supply of food for my cow; it will keep her healthy and strong." The two friends then parted company after promising each other to meet up again soon. At the small back garden, Tamun had a plantain tree, and in a small patch, a few vegetables had sprouted. He plucked a few plantains from the tree and also some potatoes and okra. He had decided to cook and eat before going to meet the village *pradhan*. Tamun then lit an outdoor clay oven with dried leaves and branches he had gathered a few days ago. Having placed the vegetables in the cooking pot, he put it on the handmade stove and went inside to tend to other jobs, whilst the food got cooked. Soon Tamun heard the cow moo, and he, suddenly, realised that Nandini was thirsty and was asking for water, so he quickly placed a bucket of water in front of her, and she quenched her thirst and sat and watched her master, as he went about his business.

Having eaten a quick meal, Tamun got ready to visit the *panchayat* headquarter. On his way out, he told Nandini, "I will be back soon; I am going to arrange regular food supply for you." The short walk to the *pradhan's* office was interrupted by a woman who asked a few questions about Nandini, as she had seen her sitting outside Tamun's hut. Dulari was the wife of the local sweetmeat shop owner; they were well known for their sweets and savouries. Tamun politely told her that he had purchased the cow at the cattle market the day before.

"Do you have any plans for the cow?" Dulari asked inquisitively. She was told that Nandini will produce milk for him, and he wished to change his profession from a farmer to a *gwala*. Dulari laughed at him and taunted him as she added, "The cow is very frail and weak; she will not produce any milk." She also stated that Tamun would be wise to sell the cow soon, as it may become a liability to him. The negative comment from the neighbour surprised and irritated Tamun as he cut short the conversation and walked away briskly, avoiding eye contact with Dulari.

Within a few weeks, Nandini had grown into a beautiful and healthy cow; she was taken for walks to the field where she would spend most of the day. At dusk, Tamun would walk back the cow to the hut, on the way, he would softly hum his favourite tune. The cow had a beautiful sheen and she had grown in size. The local people would admire Nandini, and the women, apart from Dulari, would comment that Nandini would soon produce milk. Tamun would be pleased and excited about their good wishes and the prospect of his dream coming true. Soon Nandini was milked by the local women who took it in turns to do the favour for the new *gwala*. The first bucket of milk was offered to the local people, and its rich and creamy texture and taste earned the compliments of everyone. Tamun was ecstatic as he looked at Nandini with admiration and appreciation. The cow was oblivious of all the fuss about her milk; she was happy to chew the grass that was provided to her, and provide her master with the milk he had dreamed of. Shortly, the village came to know about Nandini's milk, and Dulari and her husband, Tamlik, came to see the cow. They were besieged with jealousy of Tamun's change of fortune and Nandini's role in it, and they realised that soon the milk would be sold in the market and Tamun would prosper in his business. They were not wrong, as Nandini's milk attracted the most customers in the market, they would praise Tamun for the quality of the milk he sold. Tamun was an honest businessman, and the children in particular developed a liking for the full cream milk, and customers knew that Tamun would never dilute the milk with water to make profit. His honesty had earned him a good reputation as a *gwala*, and within a few months, he became reasonably wealthy and his circumstances had improved. Tamun's most loyal customer and well-wisher was Rahul, and as a routine, the *gwala* would give his first milk delivery of the day to the young doctor, who would wait patiently at the door. One day, Rahul decided to let Tamun know what he had heard when he followed him back from the Shorai *Mela* when Tamun had said to the cow that she would make him rich. Tamun replied, "Nandini is my lucky mascot, Doctor *babu*. I will never face hardships as long as she is with me."

Rahul smiled and said, "Your dream has materialised, and your plan for Nandini has been successful."

As autumn arrived, the village activity became less, and people would return home early, and the nights were longer. However, Rahul remained busy despite the seasonal change, and his home visits had increased. Frequently, he would pay a visit to Tamun's hut on his way back home. He would briefly stop and look at Nandini and admire her glossy hide. The doctor had noticed that Tamun's hut boasted of a few new items of furniture and bedding. Tamun excitedly informed the doctor about the new purchases from his friend, who owned a small furniture business. On occasions, Rahul would accept the offer of a hot cup of tea made with the special milk as Tamun hurriedly tried to make his guest feel comfortable. The two men would talk about their family, Tamun came to know that the doctor's family lived in Kaliput, and his parents wrote to him regularly. Unfortunately, Rahul was unable to reply promptly because of his long day at work. He felt tired by evening and he preferred to sleep early. Rahul explained to his friend that his family home was situated in the heart of the city, his brother and two sisters lived with his parents. "Where is your wife, in the city?" asked Tamun.

"I am not married, Tamun," replied Rahul. Tamun looked very surprised as it was the custom in his village for people to marry at a young age and raise a family. Tamun then was silent for a short while, he quickly changed the subject as he didn't want to give the impression to his guest that he was curious about his private life. Rahul looked at his watch and stood up and decided to leave; he thanked Tamun for the tea and his hospitality.

The next morning, Tamun was awakened by a hard knock on the door, he quickly stood up put on his shirt and opened the entrance of his hut. He, at once, recognised his visitor and welcomed him to the house. Chinmoy had a broad smile on his face, and the two men exchanged pleasantries.

The visitor then said, "I have seen and heard about Nandini; she is a beautiful cow, and you maintain her very well indeed."

"Thank you," Tamun was quick to reply. The men sat on the bed, and Tamun offered a glass of hot milk to Chinmoy, who had the good fortune to taste Nandini's milk.

Chinmoy, Tamun's *pathshala* (school) friend, brought up the topic immediately, "Will you sell milk to me on a daily basis? I have recently started a small sweet business which requires high quality milk." He then explained in detail his small business, and that he looked forward to a lucrative partnership with Tamun who was surprised and, at the same time, pleased about the proposal from his friend as he had not expected business offer from anyone. For a moment, he silently thanked Nandini, as he managed a sly glance of his favourite cow from the window. Nandini was busy chewing the left over grass as she whisked her tail to rid of the annoying flies. Chinmoy also noticed that the house was clean and tidy, and Nandini's zone was also spotless. He told his friend that he had made the right decision to buy Nandini's milk from Tamun. Soon a business deal was finalised and both men happily parted company.

As the festive season approached, the days would be busy for Tamun, and he would supply milk to his friend every day.

The sweets that were produced from the milk were delicious, and soon its reputation spread far and wide. Very often travellers would stop to buy the famous sweet from Chinmoy for special occasions, and sometimes people would place orders with him. Chinmoy too became prosperous within a few months. To add to the glory of the business, often the *panchayat* meetings would conclude with a serving of Chinmoy's famed sweet. The friendship between Chinmoy and Tamun was cemented by Nandini, and both men would take it in turn to give her a special treat. They would buy bulk vegetables from the market and carry it home to feed Nandini, and on such occasions, she would moo gleefully, pleased with the special supply of food; her favourite vegetable was the cauliflower. The prosperity of the men attracted the envy of Dulari, as she was angry that Chinmoy and Tamun's friendship had made them wealthy; she was particularly jealous of the cow Tamun had in his possession.

On a sunny morning, Rahul noticed from his window Tamun hurriedly approach the house, he spoke aloud with tears in his eyes, "Doctor, doctor, Nandini has disappeared."

"What do you mean?" asked Rahul. The two men exchanged a brief conversation, and then they went out in search of the cow. As they looked around the fields with an anxious look on their faces, a few villagers joined the search. One of the men said that they had noticed the previous day Nandini slept most of the afternoon instead of grazing in the field.

Tamun quickly asked, "Did she look unwell?" Tamun was reassured that Nandini looked fit and well but sleepy. The search ended in vain, and no one could say what had happened to Nandini. By afternoon, the news about Nandini's disappearance spread across the small village. As Dulari went about her business in the house, she stepped outside the house and looked around slyly and then quickly went inside the large shed at the back of her house; she opened the half-bolted door to have a quick look at the cow – Nandini was fast asleep. She covered up the animal with a sack and waited for her husband to return from the shop. As soon as Tamlik arrived in the evening, the couple visited the shed again and noticed Nandini was awake. They panicked as they realised that she would call out to draw the attention of her master. The previous night when everyone was asleep and the small hamlet was quiet, Dulari and Tamlik had stolen Nandini from Tamun's house. The couple had, during the day, sneakily drugged the patch of green where Nandini grazed regularly, this made her sleepy and lethargic. Therefore, it was easy for them to take her in the middle of the night without arousing any suspicion. Although Nandini had sensed the danger and had called out in a faint voice; her master could not hear her call for help.

The next day, Nandini was discovered by eight-year-old Pijush; he had heard about the missing cow as he had suddenly heard a cow's call from the shed as he played on the road near Dulari's house. Pijush was always adventurous and, therefore, he was puzzled to hear a cow's call from Dulari's shed. He looked around to see if anyone was watching, and then quietly entered the front yard of Dulari's empty house and bravely approached the back shed. To his surprise, he found Nandini, she stood in the corner; she looked scared, helpless and hungry. She whisked her tail and walked towards the boy, as if she had recognised her saviour and knew that she would be reunited with her master. Young Pijush was overwhelmed with excitement of the discovery, and ran to Tamun's house as he called out, "*Kaku, kaku* (uncle, uncle), I have found Nandini." Tamun thought he misunderstood what the boy had said, but he hurriedly came out of his house. Pijush eagerly narrated everything to the *gwala*, and they both went to Dulari's house to rescue Nandini. She was indeed very pleased to see her master, and Tamun's eyes were filled with tears of happiness, as he had lost hope of finding his cow; therefore, his emotions were great when he was reunited with Nandini. He hugged the cow and took her home. The news of Pijush's heroic deed spread in the village, and the following day, an emergency *panchayat* meeting was called to decide about Dulari and her husband's fate, as stealing was viewed as an unpardonable crime; therefore, the villagers expected that the couple would be served with a severe punishment. With a flurry of activity in the village, people had gathered at the meeting place and the *pradhan* announced that the couple would be expelled from Panchkuri, and Dulari and her husband were told to leave the village within a week.

Before the *pradhan* concluded the meeting he stood up and asked Dulari, "Why did you steal Nandini?"

She wept and replied, "We wanted to make the best sweet using the lucky cow's milk. We wanted to bring Tamun's luck to our home, as our business has suffered because of Tamun and Chinmoy's partnership, please forgive us." Rahul watched the proceedings with interest as he was joined by

Tamun, both men agreed that the punishment was right for the crime committed by the greedy couple. The *panchayat* had played its role in ensuring that justice had been served, and the villagers left the scene satisfied with the outcome of the meeting, and most of the men discussed the couple's misdeed. Rahul returned home and wrote a letter to his parents as he hurriedly penned what he had witnessed in the village *panchayat* meeting and how local matters were dealt with by its senior leaders. He pointed out Panchkuri's pride and faith in its administration and its long history of delivering justice when a crime had been committed.

****

# Chapter 6
## Cupid's Conspiracy

The autumn, white Shiuli flower was in full bloom in time for the celebratory season and almost every tree in Panchkuri showed off the bloom proudly. Whilst some were in the front garden, others were at the back. The proud owners took care of the perennial tree, and its beautiful fragrance would linger in the air for long. During the autumn and winter months, the village held a big flower market and a variety of flowers would be sold to enthusiastic buyers. Some stalls sold flower garlands whilst others sold bouquets and wreaths. Some shops also sold indoor and outdoor seasonal plants. The vendors would shout out their favourite flowers on display, and the market would be busy from early morning. The most favoured flower was Shiuli, and its garland adorned many homes. The stalls would be decorated with multi-coloured banners, and the manager of the market would usher the buyers. A total of eighteen stalls would be put up for the event and everyone looked forward to visiting the flower market. Men and women owned stalls and sold different exotic flowers of the region. Rahul was looking forward to his first visit to that market and experience the atmosphere.

Shop number eleven always attracted the most customers, as it had a display of some of the most stunning bouquets and garlands. The owner of the shop was 22-year-old Tapsi, and her husband Jhantu would be the cashier. Tapsi was a vibrant young adult; she was recently married to Jhantu from another village. The couple earned their livelihood selling flowers and plants once a week, and they supplemented their income by receiving home orders of garlands for special occasions. Tapsi was very quick with her dainty fingers as she would weave the floral adornments and other flower decorations confidently. Most of the time, she handpicked the flowers from the trees in the village with permission from its owners. The villagers fondly called her the flower girl, and Tapsi never hesitated to show her appreciation when she was called by the special name. Jhantu was not as active as his young wife, and he never missed an opportunity to have a quick nap when he was at home, and this was a bone of contention for the young couple. They would argue for a few minutes, and then Tapsi and Jhantu would soon laugh and make up.

Besides owning a skill, Tapsi was beautiful too, her dark wide eyes and a pointed nose complemented her high cheekbone. She had a beautiful skin and a figure to match. She had an impressive walk, and her soft voice was pleasure to the ears. Jhantu was also good looking, but lazy. He loved his wife dearly even though she would often scold him for not doing his part of the job in the home. On such occasions, he would look at his wife's beautiful eyes and give her an endearing smile, and Tapsi's heart would soften.

One day in December, Tapsi entered her bedroom to find her husband snoring aloud, she called out angrily and said, "Wake up, you lazy man, it is only midday, and you are already fast asleep." She did not receive any reply from her husband. Tapsi then shook her husband and woke him up from a deep slumber.

He woke up and said hurriedly, "I don't know when I fell asleep; I was just sitting and counting the money from yesterday's sale." Tapsi noticed the notes strewn on the bed. She looked puzzled and confused, for she too could not understand why her husband would fall asleep in the middle of an unfinished task. As it was a cold day, she also noticed that Jhantu had not covered himself with a blanket for that would be the normal thing to do. She left the room still preoccupied with what she had witnessed. A series of similar events followed in succession within a few weeks, and Jhantu's sleeping habit became increasingly annoying to his young wife, but at the same time, she was worried.

Tapsi's aunt visited one day and the two ladies began to talk about the village fair, the festive season which had recently ended, and Tapsi casually mentioned to her aunt about her husband's irregular sleeping habit. She also disclosed that one day, she saw her husband standing outside with his eyes closed, and Tapsi at once knew he was asleep standing. This had shocked her and she did not know what to do. Mira listened to her niece with curiosity and a bewildered look on her face. She suggested to Tapsi to go and see the medicine man in the village. "He will have a cure for your husband, there may be something wrong with Jhantu's health," she said with a concerned look on her face. After lunch, Mira left with a promise from Tapsi that she would visit her soon. She returned to the room to find Jhantu sitting upright on the floor with his eyes closed. Tapsi could feel the cold winter breeze in the room, and she sneezed a few times and felt cold. She then wrapped a shawl around her body and also put one on her husband and gently woke him up, again Jhantu was embarrassed to find himself fall asleep suddenly.

He looked up and noticed his wife's pale face and said, "You don't look well, Tapsi, what is the matter?" Tapsi explained that she felt feverish and her body ached. Following few days, Tapsi was bed ridden with the persistent fever and body ache. Jhantu tried the homemade remedies, but it did not help, and Tapsi was still unwell.

Tamun and Tapsi were childhood friends, and their families were close friends too. Therefore, it was not uncommon for Tamun to make a brief visit to the couple's home. He had not seen Tapsi for a few days; therefore, he decided to look up on her. His knock on her front door was answered by Jhantu. "Where is Tapsi, I have not seen her in the village for some days?" Tamun queried, and as he entered the large room, he noticed Tapsi lying on her bed, her head tilted on the side with the midday sun glaring through the window. She looked unwell and pale. Jhantu explained Tapsi's condition to her friend, who listened with an anxious look on his face, and he offered advice that the couple should see the new district doctor who had earned a good reputation in the village.

"Doctor *babu* will cure you, he is very good," Tamun said confidently as he addressed his friend. As Tapsi was too weak to walk to the medical centre, Tamun offered to bring the doctor for a home visit. He then left the house and walked briskly in the direction of Rahul's busy clinic.

Rahul noticed Tamun enter through the front door, "What brings you to the clinic, Tamun?" Tamun described Tapsi's situation. Rahul then asked his friend to wait and that he would make the home visit after he had seen the last patient. After some time, the two men walked to Tapsi's home chatting along the way.

Jhantu welcomed the doctor, and the three men entered Tapsi's room. Rahul took out his stethoscope and checked Tapsi's heartbeat, he then examined her pale eyes. Rahul asked Tapsi a few questions which she replied with her soft voice. The doctor took out a bottle of medicine from his briefcase and advised Tapsi to slowly sit up on the bed. She looked a little embarrassed because the house was untidy, and also because she was unable to offer the doctor her favourite hot drink on his first visit to the home. She looked at her husband and gestured to the moneybox on the side table, Jhantu at once understood that the fee had to be paid, so he took out some money and asked the doctor, "Is she seriously ill?"

"No, just a seasonal illness which will settle soon," came the prompt reply from Rahul. He handed the bottle of syrup to Jhantu and advised him to give it to his wife twice daily. Rahul sat on the chair for a while to see if the medicine had an effect on his patient, and in the meantime, scrutinised the room with interest and curiosity. Tapsi's room was well decorated with local handicraft items: on the north wall, there was a painting of the couple's wedding, and in one corner of the room, a bugle had a place of honour. Tapsi looked beautiful in her wedding regalia, with her hair tied with red and white flower, at the same time, Rahul slyly looked at her stunning set of large eyes. His attention was also drawn towards metal boxes which were stacked neatly in another corner, and the large table near the window was covered with a blue and white embroidered tablecloth. Rahul noticed ornaments and cosmetics on the table. The large mirror on the table had an exquisite woodwork frame. It looked like an antique piece and was the object of the doctor's admiration. The two men engaged in a casual conversation, and after a sometime, Rahul again checked Tapsi's pulse, she seemed to settle a little, and Rahul felt confident that the young woman would recover soon. He stood up and bid farewell to the group and left the house carrying the briefcase in his hand. His mind was preoccupied with the brief encounter with Tapsi and the effect of her elegance and beauty, and at that time, the young doctor had not comprehended that the lady's beautiful face would often invade his mind and finally his heart.

Following the doctor's home visit, within a few days, Tapsi recovered from her illness and her spirited personality resurfaced. Although she was still weak, she was active in the house and readied for the flower market the next day. She woke up early in the morning and collected the bright coloured flowers that had grown in the small hamlet, on her way, she was greeted by a few villagers who were pleased to see their favourite flower girl well again. On the way to the adjoining road, she noticed Rahul's home, and she was tempted to greet him through the open window, but she decided against it, thinking the doctor would be still asleep. She hurriedly returned home with a full basket of fresh flowers and leaves. She noticed her husband was still asleep, she put a mat on the floor and decided to sew the garlands on her own as she sat on the floor with a hot brew to keep her warm in the winter morning. Hearing the jingle of his wife's anklet, Jhantu woke up and looked at the flowers in the large basket. "You have awakened early to collect the flowers," he said in a sleepy voice.

"I had to because the market is tomorrow, and I have to prepare for it, and also, the other people would have collected all the flowers if I was late." She went to the small kitchen and made him a cup of tea, and then the couple sat on the matted floor to make the garlands together. Jhantu slowly picked and separated them into different colours, whilst Tapsi meticulously sewed through them with a needle and thread with her petite fingers. Tapsi in her jovial mood asked her husband what his plans were for the day, he replied saying that he would go and visit his friend in Shashtra, the next village. On his way back, he would pick up Tapsi's favourite fish from the market. The couple soon finished their work and Tapsi took a large piece of red cotton cloth and covered the two baskets and placed them under the bed. Tapsi heard a knock on the front gate and looked outside to find the doctor at the entrance. She hurriedly welcomed him to the room, and with a smile on her face, she asked Rahul to have a seat.

"Are you feeling better?" Rahul asked Tapsi.

"Yes, I have recovered and feel fit and well, although a little weak. Let me make you a cup of tea, last time you visited, you did not taste my special brew," Tapsi quickly added. She went to the kitchen and left the two men together in the room. Rahul watched Jhantu look in the mirror as he skilfully combed his thick black hair, suddenly, Jhantu stopped combing his hair and stood silently in front of the table with his eyes closed. All of the time, Rahul's gaze was fixed on Tapsi who was in the kitchen. He was oblivious to Jhantu's situation, and the silence was soon interrupted as Tapsi called out to her husband, "Please take the cup of tea to the doctor." She did not get a response, so she called out again, not realising that her husband had suddenly fallen asleep again. When she did not get the response, she stood up and watched from the kitchen door what had happened to Jhantu. Tapsi was embarrassed, but Rahul was still unaware of the incident. Within a couple of minutes, Jhantu was wide awake and gave his wife a sheepish look, for he knew what had happened within that short interval. The couple were embarrassed, but did not say anything, and the three adults quietly sipped their tea, and then Rahul left the hut. Once again, he was captivated by Tapsi. His social call to the house was an excuse to see and speak to Jhantu's pretty wife. Since that time, Tapsi and Rahul would have occasional brief encounters in the village market, and they would exchange pleasantries; however, Rahul had made a note of the days Tapsi visited the market, and he would look for an opportunity to visit, so that he could meet her and make conversation with her. Tapsi was unaware of the doctor's interest in her.

After a few days, as Rahul was about to leave his home for the clinic, he saw Tapsi outside the house. Hesitantly, she asked the doctor if she could have a brief conversation with him. They went inside the house, and Rahul asked his visitor to sit on the chair. "What do you want to say, Tapsi?" Rahul asked inquisitively. Tapsi was hesitant but concerned for her husband. She narrated Jhantu's irregular sleep pattern, she explained to the doctor the several occurrences. Tapsi wanted to know if there was a medical reason and if there was any treatment. Rahul listened with interest as he quickly made a mental diagnosis of possible narcolepsy. Tapsi elaborated with all the information, and the doctor whilst pretending to listen to her stared at her with admiration and awe, and Tapsi was too engaged in the conversation, so she did not notice the doctor's fixed look. On his part, Rahul felt a sense of surprise for the attraction he felt for his visitor who he had come to know only recently. Tapsi's voice seemed distant to him as he took little interest in the conversation as his mind concentrated on her physical beauty, her sweet voice was echoed in the room, and the doctor's heart filled with a longing for the young wife. He was impressed with Tapsi's loveliness on the first day he met her; Rahul was distracted by her splendour and grace, as he forgot about his duty as a doctor, and his medical judgement and obligation took a back seat momentarily.

Rahul dismissed Tapsi's concerns and said in an impatient manner, "Nothing to worry about Tapsi, your husband is simply lazy and does not want to work." Tapsi was not convinced. The doctor advised her to keep him busy and active in the house and encourage him do most of the household chores as that would keep him awake. Tapsi asked for medicine, Rahul replied, "It's not necessary, your husband is not suffering with any illness." Rahul knew he had lied to the woman. Not fully familiar with the custom of social interaction with women in the village, Rahul gently brushed his hand against Tapsi's delicate hand. Tapsi was immediately embarrassed and glared at the doctor, and for the first time, she felt uncomfortable in his presence as the doctor continued to look at her in an inappropriate manner. Tapsi soon realised the predicament she was in, and gave Rahul an annoyed look. She then hurriedly left the house. On the way home, Tapsi's mind was confused and surprised as she thought about the doctor's behaviour; her mind raced with uneasy thoughts which was interrupted by a sudden familiar voice from behind, and as she turned to look, she saw Tamun walk towards her.

"Where have you been early in the morning, Tapsi?" Tamun asked politely.

Tapsi explained to him the purpose of her visit to the doctor and asked casually, "Does the doctor have a wife? I did not see her in the house."

Tamun replied innocently as she said, "The doctor is a bachelor." The childhood friends then returned to their homes.

Finding the house empty, Jhantu was confused not to find his wife at home, he looked out of the window and saw her walk down the narrow pebbled pathway. He repeated the same question as Tamun had asked Tapsi, she told him about her visit to the doctor for medicine for his sleep problem. Tapsi deliberately avoided to mention about the doctor's over-friendly behaviour towards her, in fear that her husband may get angry, and it may provoke some unpleasant reaction from him. She treated the incident as an isolated one, and she avoided making eye contact with Jhantu. Not suspecting anything, he picked up the large empty bucket and offered to bring water from the nearby pond. After a lapse of time, Tapsi realised that her husband had not returned with the filled bucket, and she looked outside from the window, she could not see him. She decided to wait for a few minutes before she went out to look for him. Half an hour turned into an hour and Tapsi was worried, she closed the front door and went out to look for her husband; her first destination was the pond. She hurriedly approached it and saw Jhantu sit on the bank steps with his feet submerged in the water. Tapsi called out to his name. Jhantu did not reply as he sat still, the bucket was half filled with water. Tapsi called out again as she hurried down the steps, then she discovered to her dismay that her husband was asleep. Tapsi was alarmed and called out to his name, she sat next to him and waited patiently for Jhantu to awaken. After a few minutes, Jhantu's nap had ended and he realised what had happened. The couple looked at one another with a bewildered look on their faces, as they realised the danger that Jhantu had placed himself in. From that point of time, Tapsi became more vigilant, and rarely allowed Jhantu to go out or be at home alone, whilst Jhantu was pleased to his wife's company twenty-four hours, he seldom complained, except on one occasions when he wanted to have his drink.

Tapsi's worry for her husband increased with the passing days, and she did not know how to ask for help. She had decided not to visit the city doctor again. Instead, she made plans to visit Mathal, but Tapsi was not sure if he would see any patient during the cold months. Despite the initial hesitation, she took the chance, and on a very cold morning, Tapsi woke up early and wrapped a green shawl around her body and walked to Mathal's hut. She saw the door locked, so she returned home. "I will visit in the afternoon," Tapsi murmured to herself. The flower girl's plight was unknown to the villagers, as Tapsi maintained it as a secret. She knew that if people came to know about Jhantu's illness, he would not be pleased, and, more importantly, people may speculate and give wrong advice. Therefore, in the afternoon, she made a second attempt to visit Mathal and asked her husband to sleep in the house whilst she went out on an errand. Jhantu was more than pleased with his wife's instruction as he curled up under the blanket. Tapsi left her sleeping husband and walked towards the green hut. On the way, she was stopped by Tinnu. "Where are you going, Tapsi?"

"A walk," Tapsi lied. She hurriedly parted company as Tinnu looked at Tapsi's anxious face, she did not want Tinnu to find out anything, so she changed her direction and walked past the green hut. She walked for ten minutes, and on the return journey, she noticed the road was empty, with a brisk walk, she tapped on the door and entered Mathal's hut unannounced.

Tapsi covered her head with the *saree* end and offered her respects to the elderly man as she watched him prepare his medicine box, the lined small bottles were colour coded, approximately thirty bottles were in the metal box. Tapsi stood patiently for him to finish his job and then she heard him say. "What brings you to my humble abode, Tapsi?" Tapsi sat on floor and looked at the medicine man with a worried look on her face. Mathal sensed that the young woman was troubled and that was the reason for her unexpected visit to his home. He spoke in a soft voice and asked, "Tell me, what is the matter? I am expecting a few visitors soon." Tapsi hurriedly but carefully explained Jhantu's situation, she avoided mentioning her visit to district doctor. Mathal listened with a pensive look on his face and told Tapsi that he would have to examine her husband.

"When?" Tapsi asked impatiently. They arranged a date and time, and Mathal advised Tapsi not to mention her visit to anyone and not to discuss her husband's condition. Tapsi promised and left the room, on her way back home, she had a sly glimpse at Rahul's home and noticed a car parked outside. The following day, Mathal visited Tapsi's home. Jhantu was surprised to see his guest and offered his greetings.

The two men sat on the bed and the elderly ayurvedic doctor looked at Jhantu and said: "Your wife told me about your sleep problem, she is worried for you." Jhantu was surprised that Tapsi had visited Mathal without his knowledge, so he said that there was nothing to worry about, Mathal reminded Jhantu, "It is a serious illness, Jhantu, don't trivialise it."

"What illness, I simply fall asleep at odd times," came the retort from Tapsi's husband. Tapsi heard the conversation from the kitchen as she remembered Rahul telling her that there was nothing wrong with her husband. Tapsi was angry that the district doctor had lied, and understood the reason. She quickly turned her attention to the discussions between the two men in the room. The doctor was offered a cup of milk and some sweets Tamun had given her the day before.

Tapsi sat on the floor and asked, "Is there a treatment for my husband?"

"Yes, but you have to be patient and alert at the same time," Mathal reassured Tapsi. He explained to the couple that he would prepare a concoction of special herbs which grow only in the winter months; therefore, he will have to pay a visit to another village soon to get the roots. He then advised Tapsi not to let Jhantu go out alone at any time.

The winter nights were long and cold and as Mathal lived alone, he prepared his own food and slept early. "I have to wake up at dawn to go to the village to fetch the herbs for Jhantu's medicine," he reminded himself. As the village was approximately an hour's walk, Mathal decided to carry some snacks with him; he also took out his medicine container and placed it on the table next to the bed. He then retired for the night. At dawn, he heard the familiar humming bird as it sat on the roof of the hut, a few villagers were heard pass by with their produce for the morning market. Although the village was still quiet, Mathal could hear some activities from his neighbours' huts. Sibra, his neighbour, also woke early to catch the early morning bus to the town, he worked in a shop in the big city, and the villagers fondly referred to him as the city man. Sibra often bought cosmetics, costume jewellery and toys to sell in the village. On occasions, Mathal would offer him help him to sell the goods, women and children would throng Sibra's small hut to buy their favourite items.

On that particular day, Sibra and Mathal were busy with discussions and Sibra asked Mathal, "Do you want anything from the city?"

"Yes, a deep metal pan, the old one has worn off," Mathal promptly replied to his friend.

After collecting the herbs from the distant village, Mathal became busy during the week preparing for the medicine for Jhantu; he placed the herbs he had collected in the new pan and added half a jug of water and placed it on the fire. The mixture of green plants and roots began to boil in the simmering water and let out a strong aroma in the room. In the meantime, Mathal placed a muslin cloth over the jug and put it aside, a jar of salt was also placed near it. As Mathal prepared the mixture, he hummed softly as he looked at the window where the sunrays had filtered in the front room, Mathal also felt a cool breeze enter through the open window. Within an hour, the whole process of was completed as Mathal carefully sieved the content into the clay jug. Mathal allowed the runny liquid to cool under his bed, and with a look of satisfaction on his face, he stretched his forearm and sighed aloud. He then wrapped a thick cotton shawl around his body and walked towards Tapsi's house to give her the good news that Jhantu's medicine was ready; he covered the distance with steady strides and avoided conversation with his fellow villagers as he passed their house. He knocked on the door and was greeted by Tapsi. He informed her that the medicine was ready to be collected and advised Tapsi to see him at home in the afternoon. With a gentle smile on her face, Tapsi thanked the medicine man and said, "I was confident that I could rely on you for a cure of Jhantu's strange illness." Mathal departed with a feeling of content and achievement that he was of help to the couple.

As instructed by Mathal, Tapsi began to administer the medicine to her husband every morning before breakfast. The bitter taste of the concoction made it difficult for Jhantu to take the medicine, but with his wife's assurance that it would cure his illness, the young husband relented. For the ensuing days, Tapsi kept a watchful eye on her husband and noticed an improvement, the sleep incidents were less frequent and brief; Jhantu had also noticed the difference in his health. Tapsi was advised by Mathal that her husband must take the syrup for at least three months, and to come to his hut to refill the bottle and request for the medicine when it had finished. On occasions when Tapsi passed Rahul's house, she was tempted to pay him a visit and inform him of her husband's miraculous cure by the ayurvedic doctor. She decided not to think about the matter and to forget the incident at his house; however, what Tapsi did not know was that the young doctor was still besotted with her.

Not to be defeated, on the days Rahul was at home, he made a concerted effort to visit Tapsi at her home, he would carry different gifts for the lady, most of them he would purchase from the city. Tapsi felt angry and uncomfortable at his unannounced visits; however, Jhantu, without suspecting anything, would thankfully receive the gifts from the doctor, and would add, "You don't have to bring a gift every time you visit us, doctor." Rahul would sheepishly try and engage Tapsi in a conversation, but she showed little interest in him and avoided eye contact, the recurring memory of the previous incident made her increasingly suspicious of the doctor's intention. However, Rahul continued to secretly desire the attention and affection of Jhantu's beautiful young wife. Tapsi on her part missed no opportunity to make him aware of her lack of interest in his advances. Stubborn Rahul was determined to make a breakthrough, but he seldom had the opportunity to be alone with Tapsi. In solitary moments, Rahul's mind would visualise her beauty and grace. His fantasies of her increased with every passing day, and the desires became unbearable for the doctor. Often, they would greet each other on their way to the market, but Tapsi always had an annoyed look on her face, but she had not realised the extent of the young doctor's obsession for her, and that he secretly yearned her to be part of his life. Rahul was confident that he would win her heart and was unaware that the flower girl had developed a resentment towards him. Although the doctor knew of the implications of his feelings and attraction, it did not prevent him from desiring Tapsi. As a handsome young man, he was confident that one day he would be able to conquer Tapsi's heart and she would reciprocate his feelings, and waited patiently for that to happen. He decided that time and opportunity would be an important factor and he would again make attempts to get her affection. He saw Jhantu as the main obstacle and soon jealously presented itself in the doctor's troubled mind.

Jhantu soon recovered from his illness under the care of his young wife; however, the couple were vigilant, and Jhantu seldom went out alone. Tapsi was in charge of the house, and the flower business had boomed in the winter season. Tapsi became popular with her customers, and, occasionally, Rahul would visit the stall on the pretext of buying plants. Jhantu would be too happy to sell his produce to the eager doctor, who would use the opportunity to speak to the couple. His ulterior motive was to find out when Tapsi would be alone so that he could express his feelings to her. Tapsi was an intelligent woman, and she understood the doctor's intentions to flirt with her, so she continued to avoid him. Rahul did not like the avoidance, but he persevered with his effort. Panchkuri community was a small one, and it would be right to say that they were all informed about local gossip. During market days, curiosity increased and a few men had noticed Rahul's sly look and interest in Tapsi; his behaviour did not go unnoticed in particular by the elderly inhabitants. He was unaware of developments in the small village, and he made plans to speak to Tapsi when opportunity presented itself. One early morning, he noticed Tapsi go to the pond with a bucket, the place was quiet, and Rahul quickly put on his shirt and followed her to the water hole. "How are you, Tapsi?" asked the doctor, Tapsi was taken aback as she heard Rahul's voice from behind. She did not reply, and walked fast to avoid her admirer. Rahul was determined to make a conversation with the flower girl and said in a soft tone, "Why do you avoid me, don't you like me, Tapsi?"

She was again surprised at the doctor's audacity and retorted with her firm voice, "If you continue to harass me, I will inform the head of the *panchayat*." By now, Rahul was desperate to proclaim his love for Tapsi and disregarded her threat. Hurriedly, he softly muttered his love for her whilst Tapsi filled the bucket and avoided any further conversation. Rahul suddenly had the strong desire to touch the lady, but decided against it, although his mind was playing games and he wanted to embrace her in his arms – he felt the opportunity had presented itself.

"Why are you at the pond, doctor, don't you have water in the house?" A man's serious voice was heard nearby. Rahul looked startled and embarrassed, but he did not recognise the man. Tapsi was alarmed to see the *pradhan* of the village, and she quickly covered her head with her *saree* and greeted him and left the scene quietly leaving the two men together.

"I wanted to find out about Jhantu's health," Rahul replied with a lie. The chief, Ramlal, had witnessed the previous scene; therefore, he knew the doctor had lied.

The *pradhan* looked at the young man with a stern look on his face and said, "Stay away from her." Rahul was unable to conceal his guilt and he hurriedly left. On his return home, Rahul was troubled as well as frustrated – Tapsi had not reciprocated his love, and the second thought troubled him more, the *pradhan's* presence. His ego and pride was hurt; he was angry that he had not succeeded in his plan. For several days, during non-working hours, the young doctor would often think about the flower girl and his attraction towards her increased with time. At home, he would look out of the window to have a glimpse of Tapsi, as he was familiar with her routine and knew when she would pass his house, such was the extent of his fascination for her. He rarely dismissed from his mind, the attraction for Jhantu's wife, as the picture of her beauty and grace gave him immense pleasure and this attraction had temporarily invaded his temple of conscious.

\*\*\*\*

# Chapter 7
## An Unexpected Visitor

Amidst the many huts in the village of Panchkuri, Malti's abode stood out the most due to its size and its history. Malti's life at the village started as a young wife; her husband, Rudro, was a small merchant, and the couple owned a large rice field on the outskirts of the village. Their main income was from agricultural produce, which were traded in the city. The couple lived a comfortable life with their twin sons – Joy and Bilash. They attended the local *pathshala* and had many friends, and the young boys would regularly play in the nearby fields. Malti was well known for her energy and grace; many women in the village would seek advice and guidance from her, as she was an intelligent woman. In the early days of their married life, Rudro would be busy in the rice field, whilst Malti attended to the family needs. At that time, the couple had often discussed about owning a modern built house, complete with brick walls and a concrete roof. Their thatched house no longer served the purpose and was inadequate for a family of four. Their conversation would seldom yield any positive outcome, but one day as they discussed the subject, Rudro pointed out that there was a paucity of builders. Malti told her husband, "You buy the raw materials and the tools, I will try and build the walls as much as possible on my own – we cannot wait any longer to find builders." Rudro was surprised by his wife's suggestion and looked annoyed.

He replied saying, "How can a woman build the concrete wall, this is an absurd proposal, Malti." But she was adamant, and every day she would repeat her proposal, and one day,

Rudro relented and said, "OK, tomorrow I will go to the city, and buy everything for you, but I may not be able to spend time for the construction work, as I have to attend to the field." Rudro hurriedly left the room still unsure about his wife's plan, as he missed seeing the victorious smile on wife's face.

Within a few days, the news about Malti's courageous project spread in Panchkuri, and the subject became a topic of discussion in the community. However, the men were far from impressed, but Malti had the support of her friends and a reluctant husband. The raw materials and the building tools soon arrived, and Rudro was still doubtful about his wife's intention, but he was helpless as he heard Malti eagerly discuss with the neighbour. He overheard conversations as she described in detail how the walls would be built; she had also decided on the number of windows and doors each room would have. Her only problem was the roof, and she asked Rudro for advice. Within a few days, preparation for the bungalow was in full form as Malti prepared herself for the important day. As the family ate their dinner, a date for the building project was agreed. On the marked day, Rudro's wife woke up early, packed her husband's food and got ready to start her new role for the day. But as she had to empty one side of the large room, in order to build the wall, a makeshift thatched room was put up, with the help of a few local people. She used the adjoining area whilst the front room walls were built. Malti borrowed one ladder from her relative, she then carefully mixed the mortar in a large metal tray, and measured and tied a long strong rope between the three tall bamboos she had interred in the soil so that the wall could be built. With her firm hands, she gently lifted one brick at a time and placed them in a line, soon a layer of bricks had been placed on the eastern side of the hut, and Malti applied the cement mixture in between the bricks and firmly placed them on top of each other. The mid-day sun scorched the earth as Malti continued to fill the gaps in between the bricks with the metal spatula of mortar as she layered the red bricks. In the sweltering heat, Malti could feel the drops of perspiration trickle down her back; she often stopped to drink a glass of water. Her determination and confidence complimented each other. By the evening, Malti made significant progress as she looked at the front wall. She could see that the neat pile of bricks was cemented meticulously, and the front wall had taken the form she had in mind. Following days as Malti worked on her house, curious villagers would stop by and pass positive comments, as they witnessed a new chapter in the history of the village. Malti was not distracted by the unwarranted attention, and would work until late afternoon. When she was tired and thirsty, she would rest for a short while and then resume her work. She would set a target for the day and when Rudro returned home at dusk, he noticed that the walls had been raised with meticulous craftsmanship. In the darkness of the night, the couple would laugh and joke, and Rudro would often praise his wife's valiant effort. Every night, the couple would retire early so that they could start early the next day. Whilst their mother worked, Joy and Bilash would spend their time with their friends but check on their mother frequently and inspect the walls. With each passing day, Malti's dream home was near fruition as the four walls of the large room were built with meticulousness. Rudro and the twins would admire the concrete room. On the last phase of the building, Rudro offered to get help to fit the windows and door. He also promised to fit the tiled roof as he told Malti that he would seek his cousin's, Murli, help. After a discussion the following day, the two men decided to order the tiles from a local builder. Rudro then returned home and informed his wife that with offer of help from Murli, the two men would complete the construction work and the roof would be put in place. At bedtime, Malti was pleased with the day's developments as she blew the oil lamp in the corner of the room and the couple slowly fell asleep.

As the cool air came in through the open window in the middle of the night, Malti was woken by the sound of a meek purr and shuffling of dry leaves. Half asleep, she stared into the dark room and stretched her hands to feel her children; she was uncertain where the growl had come from. She quietly sat up and lit the night lamp and looked around the room, she did not see anything. She continued to sit for a few minutes, but did not hear the sound again, so she tried to fall asleep again. After a few minutes, Malti was again awakened by the same purr. She decided to wake her husband, Rudro, who had not guessed why he was awakened, suddenly, also heard the noise. The couple stayed quiet and sat up on their bed for a few minutes. They looked outside the window through the veil of mosquito net but did not see anything. On the third occasion when they heard the sound of a gentle growl, they were alarmed as they realised it was the growl of a wild animal. Determined not to attract attention to the house, they communicated with each other by facial expressions rather than spoken words. The full moon light, which had entered through the window, assisted the couple to see each other's expression. They decided not to explore outside for fear of an attack. However, quietly Malti's husband came out of the large bed and tiptoed towards the small window. He tried to see outside, but nothing was visible. They were frightened and confused at the same time, and the thought of a mountain lion cub within the hut's vicinity had crossed Rudro's mind, but he avoided telling his frightened wife, and at the same time, he did not want to disturb his sons' deep sleep, for that would become a problem. He also realised that if a cub had entered the village, the parents would not be far behind, and this made him freeze with fear. There was very little scope to draw the attention of their neighbours and Malti and Rudro felt helpless as the couple realised that they were in a precarious situation. They had an unexpected visitor on their doorstep and very little could be done. The meek growl became persistent and frequent, and as Malti whispered to her husband, she said, "Under no circumstances, you open the door, don't try to be brave." Rudro gave a reassuring glance to his wife as they sat on their bed. For the next few hours, Rudro and Malti lay side by side with their eyes and ears wide open, and the thought of the lion cub in close vicinity made the night more frightening. At the break of dawn, the growl had stopped, half-asleep Rudro nudged his sleeping wife. The pair then again slowly looked out of the window and could not see any animal.

As a routine, Rudro's neighbour Sujit was the first person to wake up in the neighbourhood, and Rudro waited to hear his voice. When he heard Sujit's voice, Rudro called out his name from inside the hut. He explained to his neighbour the night's incident and asked whether it was safe to come out of his house. Sujit listened with interest and fear at the same time and stretched his neck to see if he could see anything nearby. In the meantime, Rudro waited patiently for an answer from his friendly neighbour, and after a brief silence, Sujit said aloud, "I don't see any lion cub or other animal outside your house, you must have been dreaming, please come out." Rudro was relieved and felt confident to step out of his hut, but he instructed his wife to bolt the room from inside as he nervously stepped out in the morning sun. But Malti was prepared for any incident as she stayed indoors. Fortunately for the family, nothing untoward happened at that moment of time.

In the morning, the incident at Malti's house was a topic of discussion in the village, and everyone was advised to be alert, for they knew if the lion cub had entered the village, the parent would soon follow trail, and this would be dangerous. The *panchayat* leader advised the villagers to stay indoors as much as possible and to look after their children. Everyone was cautious, and Rudro soon left for work as he promised his wife that he would return home before darkness set in. Malti prepared to get to work with the building and mixed the mortar to give the finishing touches to the fourth wall, and unsuspectingly, she entered the adjoining empty room and discovered in a corner a small lion cub fast asleep. The woman looked startled and scared and remembered the words of caution from the leader; she sprinted to her neighbour's house with a deep feeling of fear and helplessness. Sujit's wife was busy cooking the afternoon meal, and as she noticed Malti's frightened look, she asked, "What is the matter, Malti, you look as if you have seen a ghost?" Malti was in a state of panic, as she struggled to explain her discovery in the hut. After listening to her story, the two women mustered courage to go out and ask for help. They saw the cub in a corner of the room asleep. "We must seek help before the cub's mother reaches the village looking for her offspring." Malti nodded, and they briskly marched to the leader's house. Ramlal watched the two anxious ladies hurriedly approach his house. He quickly queried about their worries, and Malti narrated the night's incident and about her morning sighting in the adjoining empty room. Ramlal's expression changed from curiosity to that of concern. He advised the women to return to their home and stay indoors. He then quickly walked to the three neighbours' huts and explained everything to them. The group of men reached Malti's house and peered through the window. The lion cub was fast asleep, and as they sensed an imminent danger, the *pradhan* advised the men to announce to the villagers to be alert and to remain indoors.

For long, the villagers of Panchkuri were aware of the presence of mountain lions a few miles away, but they have never been visited by the animal, and no attacks had been reported. The men who tended to the rice fields have never expressed any fear of their feline neighbours. Therefore, the news of the lion cub in the village was a surprise to its people. Soon children were rushed back home, and doors were locked from inside; however, the men, including Rudro who worked in the fields, were unaware of the events that had unfolded in the small village. The mid-afternoon sun was bright, and the air felt warm. Rudro was in the field checking the rice grains. The husk piles were placed near the door of a small thatched room, and Rudro decided to drink water from a pitcher in the room. As he drank, he looked outside the window to keep a watchful eye as crows were known to be a menace in the rice fields. From a distance, Rudro noticed a large brown animal stride in the direction of the village. At first, he did not recognise the animal, but soon he realised it was a mountain lion, and an overbearing fear for the safety of the people besieged the young man. The lion growled as it steadily advanced towards the populated area, and from a distance, Rudro watched a few men on the outskirts of the village already guarding with large bamboo poles in their hand. Rudro guessed that the *pradhan* had advised them that the lion may come in search for her lost cub; therefore, everyone should be prepared. Rudro became restless as he thought about his family. The large predator had covered the distance between the mountain and the village, and her angry calls increased with every advanced stride. She was angry and was in distress for her cub, and Ramlal, who stood on the main road hiding behind a large tree, was fearful but understood the lion's plight. The elderly man had advised his men not to attack the lion first, but they should be prepared. The loud cries of the large cat could be heard by everyone. The village was silent and the men did not show their presence to the animal. In the meantime, Malti became increasingly anxious for her husband, but had not realised that Rudro had decided to return to the village stealthily without coming to the attention of the lion. Soon he joined the group of men who were hiding behind a hut, as they watched the lion looking for her cub. She desperately strode from one side of the road to the other side growling and moaning at the same time. She suddenly stopped in front of Malti's empty room and walked inside. The baby cub who had heard her mother's cry had woken up from her sleep and made a feeble call for help to her mother. Finally, the lion found her cub, looked at it and gave it a quick lick with her large tongue, both lion and her offspring were reunited. The joyous and relieved lion stroked her baby and patted her with her paw. The baby lion reciprocated her mother's love with hops and playful pranks. From a distance, Malti and the men watched the emotional reunion with awe and panic.

Mother lion and her cub then graciously walked out of the room and looked around for any signs of danger. The animals were unaware that their presence and movement was being watched from a distance. The lion was relieved to find her baby safe and showed no signs of aggression or attack on humans. The pair walked out of the village towards the direction of the mountains. The cub was sprinting close to her mother who kept a watchful eye along the way. As the imminent danger had faded away, the men reappeared and grouped together as they watched the lion and her cub stroll towards the rugged hills. The large beast's growl faded away, and the villagers finally felt safe to come out of their huts. The unity of the village was put to the test by the afternoon's event, and men and women thanked the *panchayat* chief for his guidance and leadership to face the peril, and at the same time, not to harm the visitors from the mountains. They had a miraculous escape, and Malti was one of the first to run out of her hut in search of her husband. Soon the family was also safely reunited, and Rudro and Malti felt lucky that day had ended well.

Rahul sipped his coffee as he keenly listened to the story narrated by Tamun who sat on the floor of the front patio of the big house. Tamun pointed out to Malti's house, and Rahul said thoughtfully, "The people of Panchkuri are brave, and Malti is a woman with a difference; she has painstakingly built her house and was proud of her achievement, I am sure the villagers are proud of her, I hope to meet her one day. The village is proud of its panchayat and its role and its timely decision making."

"Yes," replied Tamun. He then explained that the village never had any sightings of lions, but occasionally, they would hear the distant roars emanating from the mountains. But the men who worked on the fields were always alert. To break the topic of discussion, abruptly, Tamun asked the doctor, "Are you coming to the bonfire party tonight?" Rahul looked surprised and queried about it. Tamun explained that in the winter months' full moon night, the people would gather in the main part of the village and hold a bonfire. The merriment would include folk dance performed by men and women in the accompaniment of traditional music played on flutes, pipes, drums and cymbals to celebrate the event.

Rahul did not hide his enthusiasm as he told Tamun to accompany him to the bonfire. The two men temporarily departed, as Rahul went inside his room and recalled the villagers' heroic story. He looked out of his window towards the forest and remembered a promise he had made to himself to witness a beautiful sunrise. The beauty of the landscape had mesmerised the young doctor, and he often described it in his letter to his parents. In one letter, he had invited his mother and father to make a visit to the tranquil village with a promise to make it memorable experience for them.

The bonfire was lit with gaiety as men and woman sang songs. Everyone was dressed for the occasion, including Rahul, for he had hoped to see Tapsi at the event. There was laughter and gaiety, and the night sky was adorned with stars. The full moon excelled in all its glory, and the villagers admired her beauty. Women wore bright coloured *sarees*, their hair were decorated with flowers, and from a distance, Rahul admired his lady as she giggled and danced around the bonfire. His eyes were transfixed on her movements. He was unaware of the *pradhan's* sly looks; Rahul was determined to enjoy the evening and to drink in the beauty of the evening and also Tapsi's loveliness.

****

# Chapter 8
## Wise Man to the Rescue

The large crowd had gathered around the bonfire, and as they listened to the folk songs of the land, Rahul slowly sipped the country liquor and watched everyone with awe. Some people danced to the beats of the drums, whilst others simply sat and watched the scenes. The night sky was clear and the atmosphere was one of celebration. Despite the cold weather, the villagers took part in the merriment. Rahul's attention did not miss Tapsi, as he watched from a distance; he was seated near an elderly man on the wooden bench. The two men looked and smiled at each other and soon a conversation had been initiated by the man. The senior citizen looked at Rahul and said, "Are you enjoying the evening?"

"Yes, very much," Rahul promptly replied. The young doctor explained that he had not attended any similar event before; therefore, he enjoyed every moment.

"My name is Bikas, you may not know me, doctor. I happen to be the senior most villager, and three generations of my family have lived in Panchkuri," the grey-haired man said in a casual but sober voice. Rahul's attention was drawn to his new friend, and the discussions continued. Soon he came to know that Bikas was a close friend of Mathal. As the men were keen to continue their talks, they decided to momentarily move away from the large gathering and walked towards the other side of the field as they listened to the background music and merriment.

Rahul introduced himself to Bikas who smiled and said, "I know you are the district doctor, but I have not had the opportunity to meet you, thanks to my good health!" The two men laughed aloud and shared a few more jokes. Soon they were interrupted by a young woman holding a basket of delicacies which the villagers had prepared in the marquee. Bikas and Rahul thanked the woman and helped themselves generously with her offering.

Bikas was an intelligent man, and his wisdom was known to the local people, and at moments of crisis, even the *panchayat* leader sought his guidance and leadership. Rahul was unaware of Bikas' importance and respect in the village, and as Bikas spoke, he closed his eyes and smoked from the painted *hookah* he had carried with him from his house; the gurgle sound was obvious to the young doctor. Rahul could not hide his disapproval on seeing the *hookah*, but preferred not to make a comment about its risk to one's health. The senior villager was deep in thought as he held the *hookah* and after a brief silence, he directed a question to Rahul – "Do you plan to stay here for long, Doctor?"

Rahul was taken aback by the sudden question, but was quick to add, "I have not thought about it, most probably, the Government will want me to stay for a few years, why do you ask?"

"Life can be lonely here for most single people, most doctors come and stay only for a few months and then suddenly leave," Bikas explained.

"I won't leave abruptly. Panchkuri is a beautiful village, and the people are friendly and helpful, I enjoy the job," Rahul said softly.

The two men sat quietly for a few minutes, and the silence was broken by Bikas as he said, "You will enjoy your stay more if you have a wife and family; you will live a much better quality of life in the village, I can assure you." Rahul listened to his friend's advice as his gaze trailed off towards Tapsi, oblivious that it was being watched by the senior man. Bikas managed a sly look at his companion of the evening. As Tapsi swayed gracefully and danced to the music holding her husband's hand, a feeling of jealously overpowered the young medic who stared at her from a distance. Rahul's expression gave away and revealed his inner most thoughts, and Bikas was clever to pick up the negative vibe; therefore, he gathered courage and suddenly uttered to Rahul, "It would not be wise to ruin your name and reputation for the sake of a transient desire." His new acquaintance looked embarrassed and troubled and an uncomfortable silence followed. Rahul dared not to explain to his observant friend his attraction for Tapsi and the emotional turmoil that he had experienced for the past few weeks. However, what he did not know was that Bikas was a wise and benevolent man – he understood the ways of the heart and mind. To make him feel at ease, Bikas comforted Rahul with a firm shake as he stood up to leave with a parting sentence, "You will overcome the infatuation soon, continue to carry out professional role in the village because you service is more important."

On the way back home, Rahul was in deep thought about the wise man's words; he looked up at the bejewelled sky and heaved a sigh, brushed his hair and walked briskly towards his home. That night, the doctor could not fall asleep as he recounted the events of the evening, and Tapsi's beautiful image reappeared in his mind as he remembered her body sway to the songs. Rahul tossed in his bed from side to side as he realised that his infatuation for Jhantu's wife increased with each passing day. His mind was in further turmoil as he had to remind himself of his duty as a doctor and Bikas' friendly advice; therefore, he was torn between his love and his responsibility He was confused and helpless, and wished that a miracle would happen to calm his restless soul, but the besotted doctor failed to understand that his passion for the woman was unrealistic and unattainable as it was a forbidden desire. After an hour, as Rahul tried to fall asleep, his final thought for the night was the intelligent man's advice, and Rahul was glad to have befriended Bikas at the fair – his words of wisdom was of importance to the doctor.

By midnight, the gala event in the village had mellowed down, and most of the people felt tired and sleepy. The beacon was put off before the villagers left the site, and in the quiet of the night, the howls of jackals could be heard at a distance. Holding on to each other's hands, Tapsi and her husband walked back to their home gently humming their favourite song of the evening; the couple were happy and were in love as they retired for the night. But before falling asleep, to a surprised wife, Jhantu pointed out that the young doctor was slyly observing her. Tapsi had a surprised and embarrassed look on her face as she quickly remembered everything but still refrained from telling her husband. She casually spoke and said, "It's late in the night, and we have many jobs to do tomorrow, so go to sleep now."

Bikas was the last person to leave the funfair, as he stood in one corner and looked in the direction of Rahul's home in a pensive manner. He was surprised to discover that evening the doctor's interest in the flower girl; he tried to analyse Rahul's feelings, but could not find a quick solution to help the young man. He was suddenly interrupted by the *pradhan*, Ramlal, who had noticed that Bikas had not left. The two men's voice could be heard in the stillness of the night as they accompanied each other on their homeward journey. With the shawls wrapped around their body, Bikas and Ramlal felt the cool breeze of the winter months touched their rugged face, the smell of flowers had also filtered into the night air. After a brief silent walk, the two elderly men discussed the evening's event, and the success of it brought a smile on their face. The *pradhan* was particularly happy that everyone attended, and the ambience was one of fun and happiness. Ramlal was quick to notice his friend in deep thought as Bikas' engagement in the discussions decreased. Ramlal boldly asked Bikas, "What are you thinking about, your mind seems to be preoccupied?"

Bikas was quick to reply as he explained that his thoughts were worried about Rahul. "Why, what happened?" the *pradhan* again quickly questioned.

"I hope to explain it to you at an opportune time, Ramlal, this is not the right time." Ramlal's curiosity was obvious.

As they passed by the large banyan tree, and to divert Ramlal's interrogation, Bikas asked in a candid manner, "Do you think it will rain tomorrow, the clouds looked dark tonight?"

"Let's hope it doesn't, as an unseasonal rainfall will ruin the crops," the *pradhan* said anxiously.

The men reached their respective homes, and Bikas quickly commented, "Don't mourn about the rainfall, for in some parts of the country, water is a paucity."

Following the annual fair, one day, Rahul paid an unplanned visit to Bikas' home, he was welcomed graciously. "It's a pleasant surprise to see you, young man," Bikas said in a friendly gesture. Rahul was silent and felt uneasy, a thousand uncomfortable questions invaded his mind, but he, somehow, managed to smile at the wise man of Panchkuri. For the next few minutes, the men spoke about the weather and the village gala. Bikas happily explained that the village annual event was an old tradition and was the highlight of the year, and very few people missed it. Rahul listened with interest and curiosity and, occasionally, asked a few questions.

Finally, Rahul was able to be open and honest, and spoke in a lowered voice, almost in whisper, "I have come to seek your advice about a matter which has troubled my mind and heart for a few weeks. You may have already guessed something at the fete."

As Bikas listened intently, Rahul elaborated on his feelings for Tapsi, and that it was it difficult to keep her out of his mind. He explained that the more effort he made, the stronger his feelings were. Rahul looked on helplessly and added, "I understand the futility of this amorous feeling, but what can I do, and how can I help myself?" Bikas was a wise and considerate man; he silently empathised with the young man as he understood Rahul's predicament, but struggled to accept the doctor's love for another man's wife.

Bikas spoke gently as he advised his visitor, "What you feel for the woman is only temporary and a passing phase, primarily because it is only a distraction from your side. Tapsi has not encouraged your behaviour in anyway –"

"But my feelings are genuine," Rahul interrupted.

Bikas remained silent for a brief moment, and then again spoke in his calm voice, "Try and engage your thoughts on the people you have come to serve. Train your mind to remember your parents whenever you are distracted by the thoughts of Tapsi." Rahul listened attentively to the senior man, and suddenly remembered that he had not written a letter to his parents recently, and he was overwhelmed by a feeling of guilt and regret.

Rahul nodded his head in agreement and said, "I will try and heed to your advice as I don't want to be in this situation. Although I know that this love is unattainable, my love for Tapsi seems to occupy my mind all the time."

"Go home and have a good sleep, and then start your day with the thoughts of your father and mother. You will feel comforted by their love for you," Bikas replied to the doctor. After drinking a hot beverage, Rahul and Bikas went for a walk in the village as they jointly greeted the passers-by. Rahul already felt relieved that he had spoken about his situation to a senior person and, somehow, felt assured that Bikas could be trusted.

For several days, the two men met and discussed many topics, but Rahul's main focus remained Tapsi. Bikas knew too well what was passing through the doctor's mind, as though he could read Rahul's mind and understand the unspoken words. Often, the two friends would often sit on the bank of the river and admire the flora of the area. Bikas was a keen gardener, and he would happily describe all the flowers and plants that he noticed on the riverbank, and he found a keen listener in Rahul. The bond of friendship increased over a period of time, and soon, the two men became more relaxed in each other's company. Rahul felt comfortable to share personal information with the wise man, and Bikas was a loyal friend to him. One day, Bikas invited Rahul for lunch at his house, informed him that a few family members would also be present. They agreed to meet for lunch on the weekend.

As Rahul sat in his chair on the Sunday morning, his mind was preoccupied as to what he should wear to the lunch invitation. He had also decided to buy the famous sweet from Santra's shop to present it to Bikas. By midday, Rahul was ready to leave for his special lunch, and as he walked out of his house, he noticed a group of men and a young woman heading towards the same direction – Bikas' house. Rahul did not pay much attention to the visitors and walked briskly on the other side of the road. The distance between Rahul and group had narrowed, and Rahul could overhear their conversation. Bikas' name was mentioned a few times, and the doctor soon realised that the men and lady were his friends' family also invited to the lunch. Rahul and the group simultaneously entered Bikas' front garden and called out his name in a chorus. The main door was half shut and Bikas appeared, and hurriedly greeted his guests. He also introduced Rahul to his family members, and the group exchanged a smile. They sat in the chairs in the large living room which was well decorated, as Rahul's eyes inspected all its details. He was impressed with the wall hangings and the local art and craft that were displayed on the glass showcase. Rahul looked around curiously to meet Bikas' wife, Mala, whom he had come to know through conversations with his friend and confidante. Mala welcomed everyone to the lunch. She was tall and slim and had an aura of authority, but at the same time, she was courteous and friendly. She looked at Rahul with a broad smile and said loudly, "Nice to meet you, at last, Rahul, I hope you enjoy the lunch and the company." She smiled slyly at the youngest female member of the group, Trisha, who was oblivious of Bikas and Mala's plan for the day. Rahul, too, had no clue about the hosts' spirited plan.

As the delicious food was served, the group of men and women engaged in a jovial conversation and banter. Rahul's wit was at its best, and all the guests enjoyed the young doctor's jokes and high spirit. Trisha also enjoyed the company; however, she remained quiet for most of the time and spoke only when a question was directed at her. Trisha was a shy, young woman and did not feel comfortable making conversations with unknown people, even though the family encouraged her to do so. To make matters worse and to Bikas' annoyance, Rahul did not pay much attention to the young lady and seldom glanced at her. On the occasions, he looked at Trisha, he was quick to notice her hair was tied in a long plait with a single, red flower tucked neatly at the top. Rahul was seated away from her, but he could smell the fragrance of the bloom.

****

# Chapter 9
## A New Beginning

For a few weeks, Rahul had not seen his mentor and he wondered why. Despite his effort and enquiries, Rahul was unable to gather information about Bikas' whereabouts and his absence from the village. The leaves had carpeted the land, and the chill air was a reminder that it would be a long and cold winter. Rahul's job kept him busy at the clinic and he would finish as the dark evening arrived. He saw fewer patients in the evening. On one such evening, Tapsi and her husband attended the small nursing home for a minor illness. Rahul was surprised but avoided eye contact with the woman. Jhantu elaborated his health problem whilst Tapsi sat outside in the veranda. Jhantu collected the medicine from the doctor, and the couple departed, but before they left, Rahul asked, "Have you seen Bikas lately?" Jhantu explained that the elderly man had to visit his family at short notice, but Mala was at home with a few of her family members. Rahul was pleased to know that Bikas was well and decided to visit Mala the next day; he fondly remembered his last meeting with her.

The next day, Rahul dressed in a casual attire and walked towards his friend's home; he was surprised to be greeted by Trisha with a friendly smile on her face. Rahul was equally surprised to hear her speak to him in a casual manner as though they have known each other for a long time. The doctor welcomed the friendly approach, and that the initial barrier between them had come down. Mala soon joined them, and they sat in the living room; they discussed about Bikas. Rahul was informed that he had to visit his family as his mother was unwell, but was expected back soon. Rahul listened with keen interest and asked Trisha if she intended to stay with the family for long. "No, I return home in a few days, but before then, I want to visit the flower market."

Rahul did not miss the opportunity to offer his company to the young woman as he boldly uttered, "It will be a pleasure to accompany you to the market with Mala's permission." The date and time was agreed by the party. Both the doctor and Trisha seemed happy and Mala was happier. She looked forward to sharing the good news about Trisha's friendship with her husband on his return home. Suddenly, there was a knock on the front door and as Mala looked out, she saw the tribal chief standing with a bouquet of flowers in his hand. Bikas' wife greeted the elderly man and asked him to come in and meet her niece.

The man stood in the room and looked at Trisha and Rahul. He quickly noticed the empty cups on the table. Mala offered him tea, but he politely refused and said, "I bought this bouquet for you from the flower market; this was specially ordered from Tapsi on the occasion of your wedding anniversary. Where is your husband, Mala?" He asked as he looked around. Mala informed him about Bikas' visit to his mother and then added that he was expected back in a few days, and they would celebrate their anniversary on his return. The tribal chief was invited to join in the afternoon tea, but he politely declined the invitation and bid farewell to the group. Mala thanked him and invited him for the celebrations which would take place soon.

It was late afternoon, and Rahul departed from the women's company as he repeated his promise to visit the market with Trisha, inwardly, he was pleased with the new friendship. Observant, Mala was aware of the doctor's attention to Trisha, and she did not display any signs of disapproval or discomfort about their acquaintance. Mala, like Bikas, was sympathetic towards Rahul, and internally, they had wished that he would rediscover himself and reflect on his feelings in a way that any wise person would do. Bikas and Mala had often discussed about Rahul's emotional difficulty, and they both shared an empathy for the young doctor and a feeling of family bond made them treat Rahul with kindness and dignity. Not for a second, Rahul had guessed during his two encounters with Mala that she knew anything about his amorous feelings for Tapsi, such was Mala's skill and tact to screen what she knew.

The changing season of Panchkuri was evident, and the cold weather was slowly fading. The morning air was warmer, and the early spring had cast its spell, and as promised, Trisha visited the flower market with Rahul a few days later. The journey to the market was one of laughter and hilarity, and both Rahul and the young girl enjoyed each other's company. They spoke about their family and their hobby and also about Trisha's small village. Rahul was aware that the pair would encounter Tapsi as he remembered that her stall drew a large crowd of keen buyers; she had the best collection of flora of the season, and everyone bought something from her. Trisha was quick to add, "We must visit the flower girl's stall because she has a good collection of flowers of the nearby villages."

"Certainly," came the prompt reply from Rahul as he looked towards the approaching market, but a strange detachment had already set in the doctor's heart, and he seldom wanted to see Tapsi, his thoughts about her were also less, and on this particular occasion, he instead looked forward to his visit to the flower market with his new friend. Lately, a feeling of tranquillity had replaced the previous feelings for Jhantu's wife. The changing season had also transformed the doctor's innermost feelings gradually, and the doctor felt that a blessing had been showered on him.

The *bazaar* was buzzing with activity, and sellers recognised the doctor and the young visitor. They called out to their names with the hope that Rahul and Trisha would buy something from their stock. However, Trisha had other plans, and with quick and confident strides, she approached Tapsi's shop. Rahul stayed at a distance as he looked around the other shops in an attempt to avoid Jhantu's wife. For a brief moment, the pair had parted company as they agreed to meet at a certain time outside the market. Trisha admired the spring plants in Tapsi's well-decorated shop which was very busy and noisy; therefore, conversation was difficult. The two women exchanged a warm smile, and Trisha picked her favourite roses, peonies, lilac and jasmine. Tapsi and Trisha laughed together as they exchanged jokes; Tapsi had seen the young girl enter the market with Rahul, and she was somewhat pleased for the couple. She gathered a very small bouquet of jasmine and tucked it neatly in Trisha's long plait. "You look beautiful, Trisha," Tapsi complimented. Trisha's attention was drawn towards a stem of lilacs, and as she picked it up, her mind was preoccupied with Rahul's thoughts as she wanted to give the flower to him as a token of her friendship. As she held the long stem of the purple flower, she quickly glanced around the market and saw Rahul engaged in a conversation with a shop owner who was her neighbour. Trisha reminded herself to visit his stall too.

As the afternoon arrived, Trisha and Rahul had purchased sufficient flowers and plants to carry back to their homes. As they met outside the market, they laughed together, and on their return journey, Trisha said, "It would take longer to reach home as we are loaded with our purchases."

"You have purchased a lot of flowers, Trisha. Are they all for your home?" Rahul asked.

"Yes," replied Trisha, "except for this flower, which is a gift for you. Thank you for keeping your promise." Trisha handed the long stem to Rahul with a smile on her face. Rahul was pleased and surprised as he gladly accepted the gift from his new friend; however, a feeling of guilt had occupied his mind as he had not purchased any flower for Trisha but promised himself that he would have another opportunity to do so in the future.

Mala was standing at the door. When the couple arrived with their procurements, she gleefully asked Trisha, "Have you spent all the money?"

"Yes, more or less," Trisha replied with a smile on her face.

Rahul returned home to find a letter from his parents. Excitedly, he opened the much-awaited correspondence and read the content with interest. As Rahul scanned the letter, he read aloud the contents – the doctor's father was not keeping in good health and wished to see his son married and settled. Rahul recognised his mother's handwriting, but she simply sent him blessings and had not made any demands, but did not fail to enclose a few photographs of Rahul's childhood girlfriends who had kept in touch with the family. The doctor was pleased to see his friends' photos. Mitali was particularly tall for her age, and Pallavi was as usual her smiley self. He looked at both the photos with nostalgia and reminisced about teenage life in the city. What he had not guessed was his mother's clever ploy to reintroduce the young beautiful girls to her son with a view to match making. Rahul was a good friend to both Mitali and Pallavi and he decided to write to them when he had the opportunity and respite from his work. He was keen to meet up with his friends soon and contemplated to send an invitation to them to visit Panchkuri in the near future. Rahul neatly folded the letter and placed it back in the white envelope, he then placed the two photographs on his desk and looked at them again for a few seconds; his thoughts were still half-preoccupied with the day's event with Trisha.

Rahul suddenly heard a loud knock on the front door, he hurriedly opened the door to find his housemaids standing outside holding serving metal bowl covered with banana leaves. They wore a smile on their face, and Gauri looked at Rahul and said, "We have made special food for you today because we know it's your birthday, this *payesh* (rice pudding) is made special *gur* (sugar cane) famously produced in Panchkuri." Rahul was pleasantly surprised but was equally curious to know how the ladies knew his birthday. Rahul decided to find out at a favourable time. With an astonished and pleased look on his face, he thanked the women and invited them inside the house. But the housemaids had other errands to do; therefore, politely declined the invitation and departed from the doctor's company with a birthday wish and after telling him to enjoy the sweet dish. The young doctor went indoors and sat on his dining table and spoke aloud,

"This is the second birthday gift I have received today – Trisha unknowingly presented me with a flower also. I feel lucky." He retired for the night with thoughts of his mother; he also looked forward to meeting Trisha soon; he promised himself to visit Mala and Bikas frequently.

In the meantime, back at her home, Mala was weaving a dream of Rahul and Trisha as a couple; she was confident that the pair would make a happy couple. Mala and her husband's discussion often focused on Rahul and his job, and they noticed he had started to give more attention to Trisha – and Bikas did not hesitate to make a comment. "This is a positive development and a far cry from the emotional turmoil the young man had experienced in Panchkuri, I feel happy about this, do you, Mala?"

"Certainly," Mala replied. The elderly couple also sensed that the thoughts of Tapsi no longer occupied a place in the doctor's mind, and that Rahul, too, was keen to embark on a healthy and normal relationship – be it as a friend or a romantic relationship with Trisha. Mala and her husband silently prayed for the right thing to happen for the young couple and for their union.

\*\*\*\*

# Chapter 10
## Robi's Mission

Trisha spent more time at her Aunt's house during spring, and she was happy to have the company of her new doctor friend. On occasions, she would be accompanied by a distant relative Robi for the journey to Mala's house. On one such occasion, Rahul had the good fortune to meet the pair as they disembarked from the country boat on the river. The morning was pleasant and the blue sky smiled down on earth as Rahul, Robi and Trisha made their way to Mala's house. Although initially hesitant to make a conversation, the two men's liking for jokes and laughter made their acquaintance easier, as they invited Trisha's bemused look. Shortly, Rahul bid goodbye to them and promised to stop on the way back from the clinic in the evening. The brief pleasant encounter in the morning made Rahul happy as he walked briskly in the direction of his work place. Trisha and Robi were greeted at the door by Mala's husband; he looked surprised to find Trisha arrive early in the morning. Mala was busy with morning household chores, and Trisha was quick to offer her help. The two women chatted and worked at the same time, and Mala was pleased to hear that Trisha had seen Rahul in the morning and that he would stop by later in the day.

Robi was a retired schoolteacher, and he took interest in teaching young children at his home in the evenings. The senior gentleman often spent solitary moments in his big garden and in the nearby parks. The sudden death of his wife during a hot summer month had left him devastated; Robi seldom presented with any signs of negative emotions. In the night, before sleeping, he would look at his wife's portrait by his daughter and silently say, "Always be with me, I need your presence all the more now." He would then quietly fall asleep in the large antique bed, his wife's pillow still at his side. Sometimes, Robi would be awakened in the night by the barking of the stray dogs or the hooting of a vigilant owl. During these moments of disturbance, Robi found it difficult to fall asleep again. He would stay awake for the rest of the night and plan for the next day, as he had plenty of time to pursue his interest that revolved around conservation work. Apart from his daughter, Dol, and a few village friends, not many people were aware of Robi's contribution to the conservation of nature, in particular his interest to plant saplings. His garden boasted of a multiple of plants and trees, and Robi took immense pride in nurturing them. Rahul was a frequent visitor to the garden, and Robi would proudly explain each plant to the doctor. For Rahul, a visit to his friend would be incomplete without a visit to Robi's *bagan* (garden). The papaya tree grew from a tiny sapling and stood in the far corner. Robi remembered visiting the flower market with his wife and decoded to purchase the sapling. The couple had tenderly planted the tree and watered it every day during the hot summer months. On the far side of the garden, the mango tree had occupied a place of importance as it produced the sweetest mangoes in Panchkuri. Robi had cordoned off his garden to protect it from the attacks of mischievous monkeys and other animals.

As spring approached, the village of Panchkuri burst into vibrant shades, and Robi's day would be long and productive. Following weeks, Rahul and Robi's friendship grew from strength to strength, and the young doctor's visit was something Robi looked forward to. The two men would devote lengthy hours in the *bagan* and tend to the big trees and the small plants. Unknowingly, Robi had converted Rahul into a nature lover and a keen gardener. At the end of their time in the garden, both men would look admiringly at the tall trees and their branches as they graciously swayed in the breeze. The guava tree was Rahul's favourite tree, and he painstakingly removed all the weeds around it. In summer, the tree would be blessed with the best guavas in the area, and all the villagers would wait patiently to have a share of the tree's fruit.

As Rahul's interest grew rapidly for Trisha, he visited Mala's house more regularly mainly to see his friend who would watch him with amusement as Rahul elaborated on Robi's garden. He would describe to Trisha all the details and names of the trees. One day, Trisha asked Rahul, "Do you know about Robi uncle's mission?"

Rahul looked at Trisha with a surprised look on his face and said aloud, "No, what is it, Trisha?" Trisha then explained to her friend that the senior relative had a dream to make Panchkuri the greenest village of the country and that he had planted all the trees in the nearby parks with the help of some children.

"He spends some of his pension money for the purpose, and only few people knew about his mission," Trisha said, she then elaborated on Robi's desire to plant a tree in every available space in the village, and he had approached the *panchayat* head to support him. "Robi uncle is a quiet worker; he does not announce his good intentions, but people close to him know about his love for the environment," Trisha uttered. Rahul listened with awe and silently promised to help Robi to achieve his goal.

With the passage of time, Trisha's silent affection for Rahul found expression in poetry which she only wrote whilst at Mala's house. She secretly wrote verses before bedtime and nurtured a wish to show them to the doctor at some point. On Rahul's part, he, too, became increasingly fond of the young woman and had begun to take more interest in her life. The couple would often join Robi and plant young saplings in the vacant spaces on the roadside. The afternoon heat would be intense, but this did not deter the three adults from beautifying the landscape. Robi's frequent visit to the flower market did not go unnoticed by the villagers, and some of them wanted to know more about the teacher's secret plan for the village; however, often, Robi would avoid questions by feigning he did not hear them. The spring bulbs timely bloomed in his garden cascaded a riot of colours, and Robi and his doctor friend would appreciate the beauty of the colourful garden as they held on to their watering cans. One sunny day, Trisha arrived at Robi's house wearing a worried look on her face. Rahul was quick to notice her demeanour and asked what the matter was. "I overheard a conversation between the *pradhan* and my uncle, and Mala overheard everything..." Trisha stopped halfway through the speech.

"What did you hear?" Rahul asked impatiently. Trisha narrated that a group of businessmen from the city had come to look for land in the village to build a pharmaceutical company. The *pradhan* was angry with the proposal from the men and refused to have any further discussion on the matter and told the men to leave the village and not to return. Rahul and Robi looked at each other with a confused and a surprised look, and they soon realised its implications for the little village. The men quickly added that the hamlet would be urbanised and industrialised at an alarming pace, and the natives would lose their land to the merchants of the big city. Robi's thoughts were interrupted by Rahul as he spoke, "I will speak to the *pradhan* tomorrow and find out more details." The young doctor and Trisha returned to their respective homes each immersed in deep contemplation and worries for the village they loved.

On a relaxing afternoon, as Rahul had promised visited the village *pradhan*, Ramlal. He was courteously greeted by Rukmini, his petite wife. Rahul was taken to the large back room of the house and as he waited for the *panchayat mukhya* (head), Rahul made a quick glance of the space he entered. The large walls were covered in intricate colourful paintings, on each wall, family pictures were put on show, and on one wall, a large batik painting had a place of pride. The *mukhya's* office was in one corner of the room as Rahul noticed that a stack of books and hand written notes were scattered on the floor. The absence of any office furniture informed Rahul that the *mukhya* preferred to officiate in the traditional way of sitting on the floor which was covered in a bold, yellow and red, jute mat. Having taken in all the details of the room,

Rahul sat on the floor, and he was soon joined by Ramlal. "What brings you to my humble home, young doctor?" the *mukhya* asked politely.

"There is rumour that some businessmen want to build a pharmaceutical company in the village, is that true?"

The village head was quick to explain as he said, "You have heard correct, Rahul, but the land in question is not for sale." The two men remained silent for a brief period. Their silence was interrupted by the sound of Rukmini's bangles, as she placed cups of tea and *singaras* on the floor.

Rahul smiled and thanked the elderly woman and hesitantly asked his companion, "If the men pursue with their plan, would you relent?"

Madhav was confused and asked Rahul, "I am curious to know that as a doctor, why don't you support a medicine factory in the village, although I may add that it would not change my mind." Rahul seized the opportunity to explain that the village boasts of a good clinic and the government provides a district doctor for the small population. Medicine was always made available, and during crisis period, the government had always responded promptly. Rahul further added that beside the district doctor, there was also a very experienced ayurvedic doctor whose contribution to the community was as a bonus to the people. His knowledge of his craft was unparalleled. Rahul also pointed out to the *mukhya* that a medicine factory in Panchkuri would not have any additional benefits, rather there would be a risk of the beautiful village losing its identity and be transformed into an industrial hub. A complete urbanisation of the hamlet may leave a permanent dent in the minds of the people, and they would fear the obliteration of the land of their forefathers. In Rahul's opinion, Panchkuri was a land to protect and cherish. Ramlal listened to the doctor with interest with a sense of pride, and Rahul had not comprehended that he had earned the long-term respect of the leader of the *panchayat*.

Having accepted a dinner invitation from Bikas, Rahul looked forward to the evening, and the party of men and women again enjoyed each other's company. Mala and Trisha served the delicacies, whilst Bikas and Rahul engaged in conversations varying from the weather to the latest news about the visitors from the town. The four adults relished the food cooked by the two women, and then the two men departed to the next room. Whilst seated, Rahul wanted to know if Bikas had any latest information on the matter and if the *mukhya* had made any decision about the sale of the village land. "It will not be easy to sell a piece of land in the village, that too for commercial purpose," Bikas replied to Rahul with a pensive look on his face. Suddenly, there was a fierce knock on the front door, and Robi's voice could be heard by the four adults in the room. Robi hurriedly entered the house and asked about Bikas' whereabouts. He was pleasantly surprised to see Rahul and Bikas in the adjoining room, for he too wanted to know the outcome of the meeting between the city visitors and the *mukhya*; Robi has his own motives to safeguard the land, as he had set his goal to make Panchkuri a green emerald plot nestled in the foothills of the Joba range of peaks.

However, doubt had invaded his mind as he feared that he may not be able to achieve his dream, and with this in mind, he spoke out defiantly, "I will veto any plans to sell land in the village; I will let my intentions be known to the *mukhya* at the next meeting." He looked at Bikas and then at Rahul. He was assured by Bikas that the sale to the businessmen was unlikely, and he reminded that the villagers would also resist any such plans. Robi was pacified by the two other men and he appeared relaxed and thoughtful; he asked Rahul if he would join him to plant tree saplings in the last piece of vacant land on the outskirts of the village. Bikas also added that he had purchased different plants from the market, and if the trees were planted on time and watered regularly, the bloom of red and yellow flowers would add to the beauty of the village. Rahul promised that he and Trisha would join him the following week and that he looked forward to the occasion.

\*\*\*\*

# Chapter 11
## A Summer of Discontent

The news of the possible sale of the village land had soon circulated, and people became anxious about this matter as the seniors did not want the hamlet to be industrialised. The *mukhya* and Bikas and other men frequently met privately as the businessmen from the city were persistent to acquire their selected plot of land in Panchkuri. The proposal from the city was rejected on several occasions, but the buyers were not to be deterred. The summer months scorched under the intense heat, and a feeling of restlessness and uncertainty befell on the small hamlet. The green landscape had become a ghost of its former self, as the flora withered in the penetrating heat. Children seldom played outside and most people preferred to remain indoors. There was an eerie silence in the summer air. The water in the nearby ponds and small lakes started to recede, and the villagers would go to the river to fetch water for household needs; however, drinking water was a scarcity. The *mukhya* had informed the city council about the lack of drinking water in the village, but an immediate solution was not on the horizon. Therefore, problem continued and the natives hope for supply of water began to diminish. Rahul, with his contacts in the city, sent letters and proposals to resolve the glaring problem. Very soon, his letters received attention, and Rahul was informed that water tanks would be dispatched to the village within two days, and an excited and relieved Rahul walked to the *mukhya's* office and said, "Drinking water will be supplied by the city council within two days, please inform everyone." The **leader's** reaction was prompt, and without delay, arrangement was made to spread the good news – a young man was deputised as the messenger, and a tricycle and a loudspeaker was hired for the purpose of announcement in the village. At the break of dawn for the next two days, the tribal people of Panchkuri were awakened to the sound of public message on a loud speaker. As promised to Rahul, the supply of mobile drinking water started promptly as Rahul watched men and women fill their buckets from the four large water tanks parked on both sides of the road, and traffic to and from the village was disrupted temporarily. Rahul returned home and wrote and thanked his associates in the city for their prompt action, the water crisis appeared to have been resolved.

In the meantime, officials from the council visited the *pradhan* several times. On each occasion, they offered an argument that the village would benefit from a small pharmaceutical plant which would supply medicine to the area and also generate employment. It was common knowledge to the experienced *panchayat* members that the visiting officials had political clout and would feel confident to convince the members and the villagers that the prospect and prosperity of the village would soon be reliant on an industry; therefore, the time was right to start the journey. The senior members would often discuss this issue and suggestions would be offered to challenge the prospective buyers. Bikas and Robi were the front-runners of opposition, and during meetings, they let it be known to the officials that acquiring a piece of land would meet with stubborn resistance. The three other village officials would look at each other and echo the same message, and often, at the end of such meetings, the buyers would depart with a defeated look on their face except for one man – Partha; he had made a secret plan to convince the villagers. For the next few weeks, he had made several undisclosed visits to Panchkuri without the knowledge of the village *panchayat* members. As an initial game plan, Partha made acquaintances at the local market, and gradually, he befriended a few young men from the village; he often made large purchases from the market and stacked them neatly in the white ambassador car which would be parked adjacent to the market. Partha was a handsome young man with a nurturing ambition to open the medicine plant in the village, and the plan was for him to be its first director. His manners and presentation was impeccable and had a stamp of a public school education with an added advantage of belonging to the well-known families and political leaders in the city. Partha was far from aggressive, in fact, he had a persuasive manner backed with a matching intellect. His uncle was a junior minister in the capital and had a great influence on Partha's political career. Therefore, the young budding politician and businessman was no stranger to resistance and rejection. Soon, by a stroke of luck and divine intervention, Rahul came to know about Partha's frequent visits to the village and the market. Rahul was aware that the young man was one of the bidders for the land; therefore, the doctor became suspicious. At his clinic, people would speak about the visitor in a positive and enthusiastic manner; the villagers were innocent and were unable to gauge the ulterior motive of Partha's presence in Panchkuri, but this was soon to be unravelled. Not to be discouraged, Rahul, on his part, engaged a few men in the village to keep an eye on Partha, and the *mukhya* was informed about this covert plan.

There was no respite from the prolonged summer heat, and a drought was imminent. The village appeared parched, and with the onset of seasonal illness, Rahul became increasingly busy at his clinic. However, he was kept informed about Partha and his friendship in the local community. Within a short period, Rahul had guessed Partha's intentions and decided that more effort was needed to keep the innocent villagers away from the unscrupulous businessman and politician. On occasions, on his journey to work, he would be greeted by familiar faces, and the summer heat would be the topic of brief discussions. Momentarily, Rahul would have flashbacks about his encounters with Tapsi; however, he was glad that he had recovered from the unhealthy experience within a short period with the help and guidance of Bikas. One day, an emergency *panchayat* meeting was arranged, and everyone was advised to attend.

Rahul finished his work early and walked back to his home briskly, readied himself and walked towards the *panchayat* venue. A large crowd had gathered in the open space, and the *mukhya* arrived shortly. Women and children were seated on one side and the men seated in the opposite area. The gathering was far from noiseless, as people whispered with a confused look on their faces, for they wanted to know the reason for the unexpected meeting. The three men – Ramlal, Bikas and Robi sat on the concrete bench under the large tree canopy. As the leader sat, the crowd became silent and waited patiently to know everything. From a distance, Rahul had spotted Trisha in the midst of a group of villagers along with Mala, and the couple managed to exchange a smile. Rahul, too, was eager to hear what the three men had to say, and he did not have to wait long. "We have come to know that a certain businessman from the city has made friends with the locals and has been proactive to garner support for business venture in the village," the *mukhya* announced with an authority. He went on to add, "The particular man in question has been bribing villagers in different ways, as part of his plan, to not only set up a business but to destabilise the integrity of this village…we must be cautious about this; this is the first announcement." The small gathering remained silent for a few moment as they looked at each other with a surprised look on their face. A couple of men avoided eye contact and showed no expression of surprise or disbelief. This did not go unnoticed by the young doctor.

"What is this the second announcement, *mukhyaji*?" Rahul asked anxiously. The *panchayat* leader was too keen to explain that the government had declared Panchkuri as a drought hit area, and that the monsoon rain would be delayed and insufficient; therefore, food and water scarcity would be inevitable. An expression of helplessness and disbelief was seen on faces, but the leader was quick to reassure his fellow villagers, that the government had undertaken a series of steps to overcome the difficulties. The leader had asked for additional food grains to be departed immediately and for the water tanks to remain in service until water crisis was resolved. The crowd sat in silence whilst the three *panchayat* officials deliberated on the two issues. The crowd was then informed that the *mukhya* would visit the council and inform them that he would not agree for a pharmaceutical plant to be built in the village and that the decision was final. Partha was to be instructed not to play a role in manipulating the villagers with a view to change the decision. "If someone is against this decision, this is the right time and place to voice his disagreement," the leader raised his voice as he spoke. After a few minutes of silence, one young man openly disagreed with the leader's decision, the young man was Pratik. He explained politely that he was not a troublemaker, but accepted the fact that the factory would generate employment for the villagers, as promised by Partha. His views attracted the support of two other men in the gathering. Biplab and Sukanto were educated and unemployed and owned no agricultural land; therefore, they viewed it as an opportunity for something positive at a personal level. Biplab added that the empty land at the outskirts of the village offered no benefit to the village, and Sukanto was vociferous that the barren land was not suitable for agricultural purpose and, therefore, did not make any sense not to use it for business purpose.

Bikas and Robi challenged both the men and added that the barren land could be used for other purposes which would have a better outcome for the village. "We have several proposals to consider about the land, and at the next meeting, these will be discussed in detail, and everyone will be informed," the leader answered. Rahul listened with interest and noticed that the announcements had generated a minor divide in the gathering, whilst some people agreed in principle with the *mukhya's* decision. A small number of villagers also nodded their head in support of Biplab and Sukanto. At the end of the meeting, the gathering was left with two choices to consider and support, and Rahul was aware that the village would encounter a difficult period in the forthcoming months. For the moment, uncertainty was a reality. The crowd of men, women and children dispersed as they whispered amongst themselves about the two issues the *mukhya* had raised. Some men were angry, whilst others were more practical in their approach. The view of the beautiful sunset beyond the Joba hills was a respite from the serious subjects discussed at the emergency meeting. Rahul stopped briefly to admire the evening beauty and the sunset, and as he walked towards his home, his pensive mood was interrupted by the call of his name from behind. He turned around to see Trisha following his trail. The young couple quickly engaged in a friendly conversation and decided to take a boat ride together. They were joined by Mala and Bikas and the four adults stepped on the deck of the boat and sat on the wood bench. The boatman gently steered the oar as he sang a popular *bhatiali* song. The adults were mesmerised with the evening beauty, and as the golden sun receded behind the hills, they enjoyed a joyful ride across the calm and settled river. For Rahul and Trisha, it was a memorable moment to cherish.

Following the meeting and after a few weeks, the village peace and tranquillity was disturbed with the arrival of various political parties, each with their agenda to transform Panchkuri into an industrial village. Amongst the group of men and women, Partha led the way. Rahul was informed of this on the first day, and although he was busy, he took time out of his duties to meet the political activists – the encounter was far from pleasant. The drought was also politicised, and the innocent villagers were in a state of confusion, and there was a simmering anger amongst a few of them; some men believed that not enough had been done to resolve the drought situation. Added to this displeasure was the issue about the proposal to build a pharmaceutical plant in the village, both these factors had impacted on its people. The other senior *panchayat* members became alarmed at the falsified propaganda by Partha and his associates. With the help of Rahul and other villagers, steps were quickly taken to rescue Panchkuri from the influence of the young politicians and their devious plans. The villagers were aware of the efforts of the three members to restore peace and calm in the hamlet. One afternoon, as Rahul was returning home for his lunch break, he was confronted by a group of unfamiliar men outside his home. The men stopped Rahul and asked him a few questions, and the nature of the interrogation led the young doctor to believe that the group of men were from a ruling party in the city. Rahul answered their questions in a polite but firm manner. Finally, one man instructed in a threatened manner for Rahul not to interfere in the running or decision making of the village. Jatin, in particular, was loud with his threats and intimidation as he gestured and shouted out to Rahul, "A factory will be built in Panchkuri with or without the approval of the *panchayat*." Rahul remained calm and silent, as he had no intention to reply to the threat. The group of men then departed, boldly hoisting the banner of their party as a gesture of political muscle power.

Late in the evening, Rahul made an unexpected visit to the *mukhya's* home; he was greeted at the entrance by a small boy. The *man* was seated on the floor of the back room. Rahul was greeted with a smile. However, the leader noticed the worried look on his visitor's face and asked him gently, "What worries you, young man?" Rahul narrated the afternoon incident and was surprised to know that the incident was already reported to the *mukhya*. The two men sat in silence for a few moments. Their silence was suddenly interrupted by the arrival of Robi.

The retired teacher had also come to know about the unpleasant incident, and with an angry voice, he spoke, "The village must be protected from the onslaught of political activities. Panchkuri is a peaceful village, and its people were known for their neutral views and ideas." The three worried men looked at each other in a meditative manner and were unable to find a solution to the new problem. Rahul's mind was preoccupied about the potential danger of political interference in the village and the likelihood of the introduction of bipartisan views of the local people. He knew that it would not be too long before the village was torn into divided loyalty, and its quietude lost in the ensuing political noise.

*An answer must be found,* Rahul thought to himself, and Robi noticed the doctor's expression of deep contemplation.

Robi took the opportunity to break the silence in the room and recommended, "Why don't we build a school in the vacant plot of land on which the greedy buyers have fixed their sight?" The *panchayat* leader and Rahul's face immediately showed expression of interest and happiness as if they had been blessed with some good fortune. The following few hours were devoted to serious discussions as to how the first primary school could be built for the children in Panchkuri. Rahul did not hesitate to take the lead and advised that his associates in the state education department may offer help, and he would contact them soon. The three men decided that an impromptu meeting would be necessary to take the proposal forwards. They also pledged that in the interim period, the subject of a school building should not be discussed with anyone, mainly to ensure their opponents were unable to sabotage the plan. As the long day ended and the nightfall set in, the party made a promise to fight for the school and reassure the tribal people that Panchkuri's interest and its integrity would not be sacrificed at the altar of political pressure. The doctor reached home with a feeling of satisfaction and a new hope for a much-needed *pathshala* (school) for the small village. He was also comforted by the thought that children would have their own school soon which would offer them a bright future; also, the spirit of Panchkuri would remain intact and its people, happy. For a few minutes, Rahul remained seated in the chair in his room, and a deep sense of belonging befell him, and as the wall clock chimed at midnight, he said aloud, "The fight for Panchkuri must go on."

At his home, Ramlal smiled to himself as he retired for the night and made a comment to the young boy, "The village is lucky to have Robi and the doctor as they are well-wishers who think about the welfare of the village and understands its tradition and values; therefore, we must not allow outsiders or insiders to destroy the fabric of this great village and its proud people."

\*\*\*\*

86

# Chapter 12
## Victory on the Horizon

There was a feeling of urgency in the village, and during the following weeks, the quiet village became the centre of attention, both locally and nationally. The fight for its people and their dreams was the subject of discussions in the big cities and everyone had an opinion to offer. The panchayat became very busy as its members tried to rally the people to play a role and make important decisions about their land; the majority supported the *panchayat*, but a small minority of villagers had sided with the political parties and their plans; therefore, confrontations were frequent as each group voiced their anger and frustration which, sometimes, resulted in scuffles. The battle of principles and ideologies were on public display and took centre stage, and villagers became embroiled in the politics of the land. Their reasons to support or not to support the decision of a school building would temporarily take a back seat, as most people argued loudly in public and common sense had a limited role to play. The fractious atmosphere, sometimes, scared the children as they witnessed their family members fight for their cause – the scenes that unfolded had become a sore point for the village which was known for its peaceful existence. Not forgetting their pledge, Rahul, Robi and other senior members became increasingly involved in the decision-making about the future of Panchkuri. Added to the confusion and mayhem was the prolonged summer and the drought Panchkuri had to battle with and the memories were fresh in people's mind. The government had sent additional food grains to the village, but the scarcity of water continued to be a dilemma for the villagers. Each political party took advantage of the situation and began to rumour that the *panchayat* leader and his senior members had failed to ensure the welfare of the village, but this rumour did not impact on the larger community, and soon these malicious tendencies were overlooked or ignored.

The three white government cars drove slowly through the main road in the village and parked outside Rahul's house. The doctor was expecting the visitors, so he quickly approached the gate and welcomed the senior government officials. They were the emissaries of good news. The group of men entered the doctor's house and were seated in the chairs that Rahul had borrowed from his friends. Sonamuni, housemaid, offered the men cold drinks and left them so that the important meeting could commence. The lead official was Shanti Sen. He was the Assistant Secretary in the Department of Education, his associates were junior office bearers in the government. After a brief introduction and greetings from Rahul, Shanti spoke to the doctor, "We have received your letter and the proposal of the *panchayat*. We have also become aware of the tensions and conflict about the land in question."

Rahul used the opportunity and explained in detail about incidents during the last few weeks and the anxiety of the villagers, as they did not want an industry to be set up in the peaceful village, he then added, "I support, in principle, that a pharmaceutical factory would benefit everyone, but I don't agree that it should be built in Panchkuri, as there are vacant barren lands elsewhere which could be used for the purpose… The disputed land is part of Panchkuri; therefore, its people have a right to make a decision and not be pressurised by outsiders. The government has a duty to fulfil to secure a bright future of the tribal people whose ancestors have lived here for centuries."

Rahul looked at his visitors for a brief moment and then spoke again in a polite but firm manner, "The *panchayat* has proposed for a much needed primary school to be built on the disputed land."

A brief silence followed as the visitors looked at each other, and Shanti queried, "Is the vacant land an asset of the *panchayat*, or does it belong to an individual?"

"As far as I now, the land belongs to the village, but I can check this and confirm," Rahul quickly replied. Shanti and Rahul then engaged in a deep conversation about the proposal of the *panchayat* and the possibility of it going through the process in the government department. Shanti assured Rahul that the matter would be treated as a top priority, but he could not promise how soon the government would give its sanction to build a school, given the fact that the matter had created a political furore in the state. Rahul was grateful that the officials visited within a short period, and that they had given their full consideration and attention to the account of events in the village. "I will feedback to the *panchayat* leader about your visit," Rahul replied.

Shanti was quick to reply, "We will arrange a meeting with the leader in the next few months, and, hopefully, by then, we will have some good news."

After the officials departed, Rahul felt relaxed and positive, and as he sat in the deck chair on the patio which overlooked the green fields, he saw a familiar elderly man approaching the house. Rahul recognised the lean bearded man as Mathal – who had not been seen lately. Rahul was curious to know the reason for the man's unexpected visit to his house, and after an exchange of pleasantries, the visitor spoke, "I have heard about the business proposal to build a medicine factory in the village. This matter has taken everyone by surprise, although I was not in the village at the time of all the turmoil, I have heard everything." Rahul gave his undivided attention to his guest as he listened to the senior citizen without any interruption. The visitor continued to speak in a sombre but pensive manner, "The village is older than the city. It is home to many generations, and their ancestors have lived in peace and harmony in this small village for centuries – the society was proud of its cultural and social identify. There was never any dispute or difference of opinion with the leaders who preserved every aspect of village life. Therefore, the political furore that the village has attracted weighs heavily on my soul doctor." The two men remained silent for a few moments, and the silence was broken by the medicine man as he spoke, "This fertile land provides the best agricultural produce, and although the disputed land in question does not yield crops, the need for a school is much greater than the need to build one of many pharmaceutical factories in the country. I will do my best to oppose this plan, I promise."

The men exchanged a determined look which was followed with a broad smile. Rahul thanked his visitor silently and in a rhetoric manner spoke, "Panchkuri will have its first school soon. Let people know that their patience will bear fruit. I will thwart every attempt of political oppression and dictatorship. The village will remain a neutral zone, and the villagers will continue to embrace self-rule. However, people must fight for their rightful place by holding on to their identity and pride – as they do not want the village to be converted into an industrial belt; therefore, they must continue with their effort. The rich soil of Panchkuri will go down in history as the land of growth and richness, its people the torch bearers of an honoured civilisation and the future generation as an example of hope and dreams." The elderly man looked at his guest with awe and clapped his hand. As the golden yolk of the receding sun cast its spell on the quiet village, they admired the evening ambience, but the silence was soon disturbed by Gauri, who entered the room as she placed a pot of tea on the round corner table.

Mathal had a serious look on his face as he continued to speak, "Previously, attempts had been made to open a school in the village, but it was not supported by the former *panchayat* leader."

"Why?" Rahul asked with a curious look on his face.

Mathal replied, "We don't know, but what was brought to my attention was that someone had planned to sell the plot of land to an estate agent for building residential flats; however, that person changed his mind when a few senior members of the *panchayat* resisted the proposal."

"Who was that person, and why are you reluctant to disclose his name?" the young doctor asked impatiently. The elderly man avoided the question and, instead, spoke enthusiastically about the doctor's effort and his determination to build a school in the small village, and Mathal, instead, directed his attention to the planning and the management of the new venture. Rahul was confused as well as intrigued by the disclosures by his visitor. As he sensed that it would be futile to gain any further knowledge from his visitor, Rahul reiterated with a finality in his voice as he spoke, "This time, the school will be built, there will be very little scope for sabotage, the leader is adamant about the project."

The brief but informal meeting ended and the senior man left with a feeling of hope; Rahul, too, felt a similar emotion. With plans for the next few weeks, Rahul returned to his room and jotted down a few notes in his notebook.

Next to the book was a half opened envelope which the doctor picked up with a sparkle in his wide eyes as he recognised the handwriting. He opened the envelope and read the short note from Trisha. They had decided to meet the following week; however, Rahul felt uncertain about the appointment, as he had made plans to meet the *pradhan* to request for an urgent *panchayat* meeting. The doctor realised that lately his personal life had taken a back seat, but he was certain that Trisha would understand as she was aware of the situation in the village. He then quickly scribbled a few lines in the note pad, tore it and put it back in the used envelope, Rahul called out, "Gauri, please, kindly deliver this to Trisha today, you don't have to wait for a reply." The maid hurried away as Rahul watched her run out of the front door to do the errand. Seated at his desk, Rahul wrote a report for the proposed school, he had plans to hand it over personally to the head of the Education Department, and also to the *mukhya*. For a few hours, Rahul was busy writing his report and he had not realised that dusk was soon to turn into nightfall. The room was partially dark; therefore, he put on the ceiling lights and continued to write, deep in his thought and planning.

After completing the report, Rahul finally put his pen down with a satisfied look on his face; he planned to hand it over to the officials in the village. The plan appeared good and this gave the doctor a confidence that it would bear fruition.

For the next few weeks, Rahul's day began early in the morning, and shortly, he had decided to visit the Panchayat leader on his way to work and hand over the report to him. After a quick breakfast of *puris* and *jalebis* which Sonamuni had bought from the sweet shop, Rahul got dressed and left the house, heading towards the direction of the *mukhya's* house. On the way, he passed Trisha's house, and noticed the curtains were still drawn which suggested that the family had not awakened. He scurried through the small group of men and women walking in the same direction, and although it was early morning, the summer heat was intense. The heat was uncomfortable to bear, but as Rahul had acclimatised to it, it did not bother him for long. Holding a small briefcase in one hand, Rahul walked smartly and arrived at the leader's home. He tapped gently on the door and was surprised to be greeted by the elderly *mukhya*. Rahul apologised for the unannounced early morning visit and offered to explain the reason for his visit, the doctor handed over the report to the head… "I have prepared the report for the school, and would like you to read it before I submit it to the government officials," Rahul informed his surprised listener.

Rahul continued, "Also we must call an emergency meeting this week to inform the villagers of our plans for the school."

"I will send out a message today," the senior man promptly replied and greeted the doctor as he departed.

The weather forecast for an early monsoon brought relief to the tribal people of Panchkuri and soon the heavy rains arrived with a vengeance. The thunderstorm was followed with heavy downpours, and the villagers were happy and relaxed as they realised that the water crisis would soon diminish. The onslaught of the downpour made the ponds swell up as did the wells in the village. For Rahul, it was his first monsoon experience in the remote village of Panchkuri;

his small garden and the lawn looked fresh and green; the new blooms added exciting colours to the front porch and a feeling of romance had occupied the handsome doctor's mind. Often, he would look out of the window as he watched the rains wash the roads and fields nearby, he would gently hum his favourite tunes, and during such moments of peace and tranquillity, Rahul would look at Trisha's photo neatly tucked in his wallet.

In the meantime, the political henchmen in the city garnered the support of their leaders and continued to interfere in the affairs of the village. The men were adamant to exercise their political influence in the village and as they soon discovered that a proposal had been made for a school to be built in Panchkuri; they mobilised their party comrades and requested them to visit the village on a daily basis and speak to the villagers individually and also sanctioned the use of threats, if it was needed. Their original plan was to brainwash the public in believing that a pharmaceutical factory would generate jobs and money for the local people, and the second was to negate the plan for a free school and convince the innocent villagers that it would not be a good business proposal for the village; in their view, the children should continue to attend the school in the nearby village. The politicians became aware that the Education Department in the government building had, in principle, agreed to the proposal of a school. They hastily arranged regular meetings to discuss ways and means to block the department's approval. However, the malicious campaign of the political parties had little or no effect on the decision making of the ruling government. Back in Panchkuri, an impromptu *panchayat* meeting was held and for unknown reasons. The deputy leader could not attend which had surprised everyone and Rahul. But Madhav was in attendance and so was other senior *panchayat* members and they jointly conducted the meeting. The villagers came in groups as they whispered amongst themselves. Rahul stood in one corner as he observed the proceedings of the meeting. Suddenly, he felt a light tap on his shoulder and as he looked around, he saw

Trisha with an endearing smile on her face. Her face glowed in the daylight. With a pleased look in her eyes, Trisha said, "You have done a great job to mobilise support for the school, well done." Then the couple looked towards the group of leaders seated on the wooden bench as they announced the *panchayat's* plan to build a free school in the vacant land. Most villagers had a surprised look on their face; however, a few men objected loudly as they said that a factory would generate jobs for the youth in the village, as that had been promised by the politicians.

At that point, Rahul felt the need to speak out in defend the proposal. With a calm but resolute voice he said, "The village is in urgent need of a primary school, as the adjoining villages have their own school, and Panchkuri must not lag behind in educating its children locally; they have to walk a great distance to attend school in the another village."

As Rahul spoke, a few angry men from the opposite side made threatening gestures to him, but unperturbed by their intimidation, the young doctor continued to speak, "The pharmaceutical company proposed by the politicians will benefit the businessmen and their party men, and it is unlikely that the promise of lucrative jobs for the youth of the village will be fulfilled on the pretext of lack of education and experience, and one needs to bear this in mind."

The senior citizens listened to the doctor and shook their head in agreement, whilst the women vetoed against the factory proposal. They voiced their opinion aloud and a few angry women reminded the village officials that previous attempts to build a primary school was a failure and their children had to walk a great distance to attend another school which was particularly difficult during the summer and monsoon season. They explained that a school was long promised but never materialised. Internally, Rahul was happy that the most affected people had voiced their opinion and supported the proposal. Within a short period, a large crowd had gathered and amidst the noise of whispers, Rahul bravely asked why Konso, the deputy *panchayat* leader, had not attended the important meeting? A silence from the other members followed and the doctor was unaware what had previously happened. From a distance, Rahul recognised a few men who had visited the village a few weeks ago, they appeared agitated as they looked at him. He sensed trouble and advised Trisha to return home, without disclosing the reason. As the meeting came to a conclusion, the crowd dispersed soon with the exception of the few men who slowly walked towards the doctor. One of the men addressed Rahul politely, and was quick to add that the young men in the village needed jobs and the medicine factory would have provide them the opportunity. As the speaker gave his unsolicited opinion, the doctor felt slightly intimidated, and hurriedly left the scene without a reply. His mind was still preoccupied about the meeting and deputy leader's absence.

As Rahul walked briskly back to his home, he noticed Konso walking from the direction of the train station. Rahul waited to speak to the senior member. As the two men met half way down the road, the doctor greeted Konso and queried about his welfare. The elderly man looked awkward and avoided any question about the matter. He did not give an explanation as to why he had not attended the meeting in the afternoon, this, therefore, further puzzled Rahul. After an exchange of greetings and pleasantries, the two men parted company, with Rahul leading the way ahead.

Panchkuri was abuzz with the news of the school, and most of the villagers were pleased about the development in the village. The children were excited at the prospect of attending a school in their own village; however, a few of them were sad because they would not see their friends in the old one. Within a few weeks, preparations were made for the building work to start. One day, a couple of senior women visited Konso's house with a request to find a suitable date for the function for the laying of the foundation stone for the school. They were disappointed, as he informed them that he would be away for a few weeks to attend to some family matters, and that the women should approach the other senior members. The women then discussed the matter with Rahul who was also surprised to be informed that Konso would not be present at the significant ceremony. The doctor promised to speak to other members to decide a date. Soon a date for the big event was announced, and it was agreed to arrange a meeting with other members. Instructions were circulated in the village so that preparations were underway, and the doctor was excited and pleased that finally everything was falling into place; however, occasionally, the thought of Konso's absence and his lack of interest in the developments in the village perplexed Rahul. Konso had not made effort to attend any meetings, and his indifference to the plan made the doctor wonder about many possibilities.

When spoken to by other members, the deputy leader had avoided the subject giving various excuses which included family problems, but the senior members were far from convinced as they remembered what had happened in the past and had suspected Konso's role in sabotaging the plans for the village. Rahul had also noted the change in Konso's behaviour and interest. The doctor sensed something was unusual and decided to find out what had happened, but it was not a priority for Rahul at that moment of time, as other important matters needed urgent attention.

On an early autumn morning, the village was awakened to the sound of bugles and drum beats, as a procession of men and women walked slowly towards the building site. The large branches on the trees swayed gently in the breeze, whilst the birds echoed their tunes for all to hear. The women wore colourful *sarees* and had their hair pinned to small white jasmines. The mood in the village was one of carnival as men skipped, sang and danced to the beat of the drums. The children had an excited look on their face and ran ahead of the crowd to occupy the most advantageous place at the site. Ramlal proudly led the large congregation as the doctor followed the crowd with a triumphant look on his handsome face. He looked sideways to his girlfriend who whispered in his ears and told him, "Malti has been given the honour to lay the foundation stone, and I am sure you know the reason why."

"That's wonderful news, it's fair that the first woman builder in the village should be given a place of honour at this momentous event," Rahul replied with a smile on his face. He then stretched his neck to identify the important woman, Malti, who was in the crowd, the procession of men and women was greeted by visitors – and Rahul could see that the news of the occasion had spread beyond the boundaries of Panchkuri.

Rahul was soon joined by Mathal as he added, "This would not have been possible without you, Rahul… The much needed school is now a reality." The two men and Trisha silently walked together for the next few minutes as they watched the crowd witness the historic moment.

The large crowd had arrived at the location, and the area was decorated with flowers and festoons. Rahul watched Malti, wearing a red and white cotton *saree*, as she stepped forwards, she sang a popular local song and was soon joined by a chorus of men and women, she then tunnelled the soft earth with a spade in her hand. She gently lowered the spade to the beats of the drum as she sang aloud with the crowd as her cheerleader. She looked happy and proud, for she recognised the importance of the event, occasionally, she smiled at the people, and she guessed that her most ardent supporter was the young doctor in the large crowd, as she heard his baritone voice sing loud the familiar song. The *panchayat* leader clapped his hands in delight, and he was soon joined by men, women and children. For a few minutes, everyone's eyes were transfixed on the unfolding scene, and one man could be heard shouting out loud to the crowd to join in the singing. Different drumbeats also could be heard, but the sound of bugles was the loudest. A group of women in a corner lifted their head quietly looking up at the sapphire sky as they blew the white conch shell to usher in the auspicious moment. Children clapped their hands in joy and gaiety, and the senior members looked on to the proceedings of the morning. Having tunnelled deep into the soil, Malti placed the bricks in a line and slowly filled its crevice with mortar, as her firm but gentle hands caressed the lined bricks. She was offered help with the job, but as she was a confident person, she decided to complete the task on her own. A soft southerly wind had briefly stopped its journey over Panchkuri, and the sun was bright, and there were no signs of a downpour. Shortly, the foundation stone was laid with mortar and brick and a few men and women helped the lady to wash her hands and her bare feet. As she cleaned herself, she looked at the new construction with a smile, and recollected her first experience as a woman builder a few years ago. She remembered fondly about the time she built the house based on her determination and hard work; her mind was also preoccupied with thoughts of the four-legged visitors from the mountain and their missed encounter with the petrified villagers; however, Malti was unaware that her story had been narrated to the doctor and that she had earned his respect. Conscious that everyone was watching her, Malti's mind quickly returned to the present moment as she thanked the *panchayat* leaders for bestowing the honour to her to lay the foundation stone of the village school; she beamed and looked triumphed and satisfied as she waved her two hands and smiled to the crowd.

As it was lunchtime, the gathering waited patiently for the caterers to arrive, and children in particular were hungry and were curious to know about the mid-afternoon meal. Rahul could see the large brown catering van approach the location, and soon, preparations were made to distribute the food packets to everyone. With the van parked away from the crowd, Rahul unlocked its backdoor and announced for children to be served first. The youngest member of the crowd, three-year-old Rukmini, led the way, as Rahul handed over the first large food packet to her, as her mother looked on. Rukmini opened the packet and gleefully shouted out aloud, "Wow, *singaras*, *sandesh*, *nimki*, more *sandesh*." – She held the packet and disappeared in the crowd with her mother. The other men joined Rahul to distribute the packets to the crowd who formed a line in front of the van. The *panchayat* had made good preparations for the event as they knew that food would be an important aspect of the occasion; therefore, every effort was put in to select the favourite savoury items.

The chosen caterer was a well-known entity from the next village, and there was sufficient food for everyone. The nearby tube well provided the crowd with drinking water in the afternoon heat. As the crowd dispersed, Rahul was pleased with the event of the day and briefly glanced at the foundation stone, convinced that the school building would be completed soon, and the children would have their own place of education. With happy memories of the eventful day, he and Trisha slowly walked away from the fading crowd towards the direction of their respective homes.

****

# Chapter 13
## A Letter Arrives

The winter spell continued and for most part of the season, the village was host to a number of outdoor activities as the period offered a much-awaited respite from the summer heat and the deluge of the monsoon rains. Men and women alike toiled in the nearby fields, and in the evenings when they returned home, the families would sit near a bonfire and talk about matters of common interest. One winter morning, as Rahul was about the leave for work, the postman delivered an urgent brown envelope, and with a surprised look on his face, the doctor opened the mail and read it. Whilst reading his expression changed from surprise to sadness. It was a transfer letter which Rahul had not expected, as his tenure as the District Doctor of Panchkuri was for two years, with the possibility of it being extended. Rahul sat in the chair near the window, and with a pensive look on his face spoke out aloud, "Why this early transfer to the city?" And, of course, he did not know the answer, but promised to find out more. He put the letter on the writing bureau and left for the clinic, still confused about the morning delivery and the sudden news.

On reaching the small hospital, he noticed a large gathering outside. They were waiting for Rahul to arrive. During the midweek, the crowd was larger; therefore, to Rahul, the scene was not unusual, except that he recognised one man who had visited the village on previous occasions when the subject of a school building was discussed at a panchayat meeting. However, Rahul proceeded to examine the women patients in an orderly manner, following which a senior male patient approached the doctor with an ear infection.

As Rahul scrutinised the bleeding right ear, he heard the man whisper, "We will miss you when you leave the village, doctor." Rahul stopped momentarily with a look of disbelief on his face. He pondered how the elderly man had come to know about his sudden transfer from Panchkuri, but decided not to engage in a conversation with his patient. The silence between the two men was uncomfortable, but they understood the reason for it. The outdoor patient clinic was busy, but with the assistance of the male nurse, Rahul successfully examined and treated all the villagers, which included a few children. On leaving, each adult patient glanced at the doctor with a sad smile, almost suggesting that they, too, were aware of his predicament. The women in particular were sad as they valued his medical skill and knowledge, and they realised that the village would lose their favourite doctor soon. The last man to see Rahul was the experienced medicine man, Mathal, but he did not come as a patient, but to speak to Rahul privately. It was past midday, and the clinic had finished, and the two men went inside an adjoining room. The elderly man spoke first and said, "We know that you will be leaving Panchkuri soon, the man with the blue shirt in the crowd hinted this morning."

"How did he know?" Rahul promptly asked. It was explained to him that the bigwig politicians were unhappy about the land not being allocated for a pharmaceutical company and that the young doctor was the main target of their discontent and grudge and was possibly the reason for Rahul's early transfer back to the city; Mathal went on to explain that that well-named politicians had jeopardised many plans the *panchayat* leaders had proposed previously.

"The government building is the centre of bureaucracy and political interference," Mathal spoke again. Rahul was deeply saddened that his and other villagers' good intentions for the village and for the children had become a sour point for opportunistic politicians.

With a heavy sigh and with an unhappy look on his face, Rahul replied to the medicine man, "The children will be proud to of their new school and will hold on to their memories of their education in the first school of the village. The villagers will also remember with nostalgia that they had battled bravely for a common cause and witnessed its fruition. Before I leave, I hope I have the opportunity to meet the teachers from the local area."

The following remaining weeks was a busy period for the Rahul as he completed all the paperwork and arranged the final medical care for his friendly patients. Trisha was upset and sad about the news of her friend's imminent departure from the village. During the following weeks, the couple met frequently and shared happy moments together, but the thought of leaving her behind made Rahul sad. He had recognised that the intimate feelings were mutual and reciprocal. It was cemented with love and bond, and the couple shared common interests which included the welfare of Panchkuri. As an optimistic man, Rahul was prepared to make important decisions about his personal life and decided to inform his parents. Late one night, he gathered courage and wrote a short letter to his parents, advising them to be ready to welcome Trisha to the family as their daughter-in-law as he had made a decision to marry the woman he loved. The letter was posted in the morning. The following day, Rahul approached Trisha's house in the next village and knocked briskly on the front door. He was greeted by Trisha's mother, who immediately recognised the doctor from Panchkuri. She smiled and welcomed him inside. She ushered Rahul to the inner rooms of the large two-storeyed house. Rahul smiled back at the small family as he entered the spacious courtyard. Two gentlemen, Anup and Dev and a surprised Trisha who were seated looked at their guest, whilst the women continued with their morning household errands. Rahul briefly introduced himself and sat on one of the vacant chairs. Trisha introduced her father, Vishwas, to her friend, and the two men began a polite conversation. Not knowing the reason for Rahul's unannounced visit to the house, Trisha left the courtyard with a puzzled look on her pretty face. As she left, Rahul asked her father, "Is it possible to speak to you in private?"

"Certainly, let us go to the office room," Vishwas answered. Other members of the household looked at the two men as they left the scene.

The short conversation between Rahul and Vishwas was fruitful and a joyous occasion. Rahul had asked the senior gentleman's permission to marry his daughter. Vishwas knew he could not have asked for a more suitable boy for his only daughter, despite knowing that she would move with Rahul to the city and Vishwas would see less of her. He remembered the frequent mention of Rahul's name during conversations with his daughter, and had half guessed that theirs was a special relationship; therefore, he did not hesitate to the marriage proposal from Rahul as he was confident that the couple would be happy together. Inwardly, he blessed Trisha and Rahul, and he announced the good news to the extended family members; the family did not miss the opportunity to share the important news beyond the boundaries of Trisha's home. Therefore, it was not too long when extended family members arrived in groups with sweets and flowers as gifts for the couple. As Rahul had planned to take the day off from work, he was not in a hurry to return; therefore, he gladly accepted the lunch invitation. In the meantime, Ruplekha, Trisha's mother made hasty preparation for the impromptu engagement ceremony which she announced proudly would be held in the evening before dusk and before Rahul returned to Panchkuri. In the adjoining room, Trisha sat on the four-poster bed with a blushed look on her face and was surprised at the turn of events, but she secretly loved every moment. She felt blessed and happy that Rahul would be her dream husband, as she had secretly nurtured a desire to marry him. She had come to know him intimately and loved and respected him for his endearing qualities and dedication to work in the small village. She remembered she had often discussed Rahul with her friends, but never revealed to them the extent of her affection for him – that had remained a secret.

Before dusk, the party of men and women gathered in the large hall, a few children skipped in the courtyard, oblivious of the significant event in their aunt's life. Despite the short notice, guests had arrived on time to witness the joyful event as Ruplekha gently brought her daughter to the centre of the hall. Trisha looked magnificent in a yellow *Banarasi saree* with matching yellow flowers neatly tucked in hair. She gave a sly look at her would-be-husband, as a besotted Rahul looked at the woman who had stealthily stolen his heart. The brief ceremony was conducted with precision as Rahul placed a gold ring on Trisha's dainty finger. The same procedure was followed for Rahul. He had purchased Trisha's gold ring from the village jeweller. The sound of conch shells heralded the occasion and it filled the air as a few men played the drums. The oil lanterns were prepared to be lit to enhance the decoration of the hall. As darkness fell upon the quiet village – the sound of laughter and merriment was noticeable, and the smell of delicious food added to the jollity. Waiting patiently, each senior family member blessed the couple, whilst the children giggled and made funny jokes which only they understood. After a sumptuous dinner and as the night sky reminded everyone about the late evening, , the crowd began to disperse, and Rahul too decided to return home; he walked to the front door and was followed by Vishwas who was keen to ensure that Rahul had a safe return journey. Vishwas did not want him to return home alone in the dark; therefore, instructed his nephew to accompany the doctor and stay overnight at his relative's house in Panchkuri. The two men departed soon, and after an hour, they reached Panchkuri, and as the doctor approached his house, Rahul was suddenly confronted by the same man he had seen at his clinic a few weeks ago. The stranger held a torch in his hand and looked threatening and aggressive, as if an open invitation to conflict was offered; he shouted at Rahul, blamed him for the loss of an industry and that Rahul would regret his actions. The young doctor was quick to understand the reason for the stranger's anger which was directed at him. Rahul's companion looked on helplessly and dared not to intervene.

With a menacing look on his face, the aggressor disappeared in the darkness of the night as he promised to harass the doctor for the remaining days in the village. Although he was afraid, Rahul appeared calm and without replying, he and his acquaintance continued with the remainder of their journey, occasionally turning back to see if they were being followed. In a soft but firm voice, Rahul advised his companion not to react if they were approached again, but fortunately, the journey ended without any further incidents as the men finally reached their home. As Rahul prepared to retire for the night, his thoughts were preoccupied with the day's event and the encounter with an agitated man on his return journey home. With a meditative look on his face, Rahul lay on his bed and recollected that the deputy *panchayat* leader had not been seen or involved in the activities of the village lately. His thoughts preoccupied, and he remembered Konso's initial enthusiasm about the school project. Therefore, Rahul was suspicious about the leader's absence on the special occasion in the village a few weeks ago. Rahul had a strange feeling about everything, and as he switched off the table light and turned sideways to fall asleep, he remembered Trisha and with a smile on his lips, Rahul fell asleep – his last thoughts of the day was of his fiancée.

\*\*\*\*

# Chapter 14
## The Sweet Sound of *Shehnai*

Trisha was excited and at the same time surprised about her sudden change of fortune, but looked forward to the wedding and to a new life in the city with her new family. Her household was the centre of activity for the important day which was arranged by Rahul's parents. Both the families had agreed the marriage to be solemnised in two weeks' time. Trisha was nervous about meeting her in-laws the following day as her mother (Ruplekha) had invited them for the *ashirbad* (blessing) ceremony. On receiving their son's letter and the good news, Rahul's parents had arrived at Panchkuri without delay, they were keen to meet their daughter-in-law and any procrastination would not be welcomed. Rahul, his parents and a small party of men and women departed for Trisha's home early in the morning; their plan was to bless the new would-be-bride and spend the day in merriment and laughter at her house. Before leaving the house, Moitri Devi, Rahul's mother, instructed the two ladies in waiting to put the luggage in the house. She hurriedly checked her large handbag for the gold necklace, which Rahul's grandmother had given her when she was married to the Bagchi family fifty years ago.

The morning was bright and pleasant, and the long journey in the car did not spoil the party's good mood. The ride was bumpy and slow, but with an experienced driver, Rahul was confident that they would reach Trisha's home on time. As the car slowly passed through main narrow road of Panchkuri, the villagers greeted them, and Rahul courteously acknowledged their greetings as he waved at the passers-by.

Suddenly, the driver had to slow down the car as the passengers noticed a group of agitated men holding placards in the middle of the road. There were shouts of anger and protest, and Rahul managed to pick up a few words about the new school; he noticed the leader to be the same man he had encountered during his previous return journey from Trisha's house. Rahul was certain that the young man was the mastermind behind all the troubles he had encountered. The young man stood on a small stool as he addressed a group of men standing next to him, "We need business in the village and not a school," the man shouted aloud, as he continued in an angry tone, "the idea of a village school was the brainchild of the doctor; he should not have been allowed to be involved in the *panchayat's* meetings as he has influenced most of the senior members to make a decision in favour of a primary school rather than a small industry which Panchkuri desperately needs." Rahul noticed the angry man clench his fist and point towards the stationary car at a distance. The doctor also noticed a few men obstructing the road with wooden rods. The man instructed his followers to surround the car and question the doctor. Rahul slowly understood the seriousness of the situation and the difficulty he had placed his parents in. As he saw the small crowd approaching his car, he stepped out slowly and advised the driver to lock the doors; the doctor could hear his mother pleading with him not to confront the group of men waiting outside the car. A thousand thoughts had invaded Rahul's mind, as he prepared himself to face and talk to the angry crowd. As he looked at the crowd, the doctor briefly noticed Konso, the deputy leader at a distance; he wore a guilty look on his face, but Rahul did not make the connection to the present situation. The elderly leader quickly disappeared to avoid any question.

For many years, Rahul had mastered the skill of negotiations in difficult situation, so he spoke to the angry man with a gentle but firm voice, "You had confronted me a few days ago and accused me of sabotaging the business offer from the city, but my role in this matter was minimal. I offered advice about the necessity of a village school."

"You say a lie, doctor, we know your influence was the main reason, you should have remained an outsider in Panchkuri and not get involved in its affairs," the stranger replied and as he came in close proximity to Rahul, the doctor took a back step to avoid any physical threat from the man.

With an angry look on his face, the agitated man thrust his closed fist in front of Rahul's face as a gesture of physical violence; however, he was immediately stopped by Soren, the station guard Rahul had befriended when he first arrived at the village. Rahul was relieved to see Soren and thanked him for his intervention. Soren spoke with a determined voice, "Leave the doctor alone... You must not blame him for anything – if you attack him or the passengers, I will not hesitate to call the police officer; therefore. I advise you to leave immediately."

The small crowd had sensed danger and the mention of Police had an immediate impact and the young man; he softened his voice, but continued to argue on various matters which did not make any sense to Rahul. With a wave to the driver and a feeling of unease, the doctor boarded his car for the onwards journey hoping that no further untoward event would take place. He could see the group of agitators walk away from the scene, as they whispered with each other, and occasionally, the main leader could be seen looking at the car. The flapping placards were placed in a bag and swiftly taken away by a cyclist.

The delayed arrival at Trisha's house had to be explained by the reluctant doctor; however, Trisha's father had concerned look on his face as Rahul narrated the incident. As the mid-noon sun glared in the blue sky, guests started to arrive for the ritual, and some of Trisha's friends entered her room. Wearing a pink silk *saree* with her hair tied into a loose plait, the young bride-to-be looked elegant, and she slipped the large gold bangle into her right hand which her grandmother had gifted to her. She sat on the bed near the window, and the sun light heightened the young woman's beauty as her blushed face stared at the mirror. Her friends took it in turns to make her feel coy and amused her as they joked and laughed in the large room. The household was abuzz with activity and the smell of delicious food made people hungry – the excitement was at a fever pitch. The blessing ceremony was the beginning of a grand seven-day wedding celebrations.

The large reception hall was decorated with flowers purchased from the flower market and adorned by the flower girls of the two villages. As Trisha entered the room, there was silence and Moitri Devi looked at her daughter-in-law with admiration and love. Slowly, Trisha sat in the large chair surrounded by her family. After a brief conversation, Moitri Devi opened her fashionable bag and took out a large red velvet box. The onlookers waited patiently to get a glimpse of the gold necklace, which Rahul's mother gently placed on Trisha's neck. The bulky but beautiful necklace with intricate filigree work was a family heirloom and had been passed down for three generations. Rahul looked at his bride with a sense of pride and fulfilment as he watched his parents bless Trisha and welcomed her to the Bagchi family.

The wedding day arrived soon and Panchkuri and its neighbourhood villages were in celebratory mood... The good news had spread far, and despite the minor glitches, the preparation was successful. However, Rahul's mind would, sometimes, wonder off as he thought about the two previous incidents, and wondered if anything sinister was brewing in the village. He had invited all the *panchayat* committee members, including its deputy leader. On the big day, the sweet sound of *shehnai* could be heard at Trisha's house, and everyone was in a triumphant mood, and expressions of happiness was evident everywhere.

The local priest had completed the wedding ceremony on time, and by late evening, Rahul and Trisha were announced as husband and wife. The Bagchi family again welcomed their new member, and Rahul's parents were particularly delighted about their son's significant other. The night sky was beautiful and a solitaire diamond star could be seen in the sky as a celestial witness to the event. Guests arrived in large numbers, and the sound of joy and laughter filled the air, and dancing and singing formed part of the evening. The young married couple looked blissful and happy as they sat on the dais constructed for the special occasion.

The wedding was a big success, and its organisation was the talk of the village. The following day in the evening, the Bagchi family with their new member departed in the big car which was followed by another small car carrying Trisha's belongings. With a loving caress to her family members, the young bride bid farewell as she mentally prepared for her new life. Although she was sad to part from her family, Trisha accepted her new role in the Bagchi family.

Within a few days, Rahul's mother and his wife became good friends, and Moitri Devi enjoyed her daughter-in-law's company. They made preparations to leave for the city as Rahul had been busy completing all the outstanding jobs and handing over the responsibility to the new doctor who had arrived a few days earlier. Two days prior to their departure, the young doctor made farewell visits to the many homes he had known well; however, the deputy *panchayat* leader's home was locked from outside. Rahul marched towards Mathal's home to bid him goodbye. The ayurvedic expert noticed the young doctor approaching his home and quickly greeted him. The two men sat on the outside bench as they talked on various matters, and during their brief conversation, the deputy leader's absence was mentioned. Rahul was surprised to discover Mathal's obvious dislike and mistrust of Konso and he soon understood the reason for the dislike. The following conversations with Mathal revealed a secret about the deputy leader's previous misdeeds which other *panchayat* members had not known. Mathal went on to explain to Rahul that Konso was responsible for sabotaging a plan for a school building a few years ago; he was part of the cesspool of political corruption which had emanated from the big city and, therefore, they had an influence over their decision in respect of Panchkuri. Mathal knew that the deputy wanted to change Panchkuri's self-rule and, instead, be governed by the state machinery, so that industries could be promoted with an ulterior motive to enhance his personal financial situation.

Therefore, for a long time, Mathal was dismissive of the intentions of the deputy leader and the lack of his honest leadership, which Rahul was quick to fathom out. Without making any comment on the matter, the young doctor recalled and informed Mathal of the two unpleasant incidents. The medicine man nodded his head and said, "You will discover certain truths when you return to the city." And without elaborating further, he simply smiled and looked at his guest. The two men briefly exchanged a glance, but Rahul's mind was racing with odd thoughts and presumptions. Mathal requested for the doctor's address which Rahul promptly obliged, and then he left with a feeling of goodwill for the medicine man whom he had befriended during his stay in the village.

As the morning fresh air greeted the village, Rahul and his family prepared to leave for the station. A large crowd had assembled outside his home and as gesture of gratitude and goodwill, many villagers had brought small gifts for their favourite doctor. A few people also thanked Rahul for making their dream project of a school possible. With a sad look on his face, and with folded hands, Rahul invited the villagers to visit his home in Kaliput. As he spoke gently, he said, "I will treasure the fond memories of Panchkuri and promise to visit the village regularly. I will remember all my friends and your affection." He had fathomed that his untimely transfer was the result of a political vendetta against him orchestrated by Partha and a few disgruntled villagers. He boarded the parked white ambassador car, and as it drove away, Rahul and Trisha looked behind for the last time to see the people wave goodbye to their well-wishers. For Rahul, the return train journey to the city would be an opportunity to reflect on the events of the last few weeks in Panchkuri, the village he had made his home and its people who had welcomed him with an open heart.

# Epilogue

On his return to his hometown of Kaliput, Rahul discovered that very little had changed in the city, and he became busy adjusting to his new married life and the new job in the big busy hospital. Trisha's first-hand experience of urban life was very different to the one she had lived in her village. Therefore, she had to adapt to her new family and the social life they were accustomed to. The Bagchi household was busy and noisy and all its members carried a happy and content demeanour. Moitri Devi was always the first point of contact when Trisha wanted queries to be answered. The happy chatter of women in the house was the highlight of everyday life, and Trisha as the youngest member attracted most of the attention. The young bride soon made friends in the local community also.

The departure of Rahul from Panchkuri was welcomed by a few villagers, which included Konso, deputy *panchayat* leader, which Rahul had discovered during his frequent visits to the small village. The newly married couple would make short trips to the village, and they stayed at Trisha's house. During such trips, Rahul would make social visits to most of his acquaintances in the village – to the doctor, Panchkuri was still his home. During his frequent visits to the village, Rahul had noticed the changes in the small and quiet village. Although the building of the village school had progressed well, he had noticed, on the outskirts, large billboards of potential housing estates inviting residents from the city. A few plots of land were already sold for multi-storey buildings, and Rahul was informed by the senior villagers that most of the adjoining land was sold to promoters for building of residential homes and other small-scale industries. They complained to him that a few villagers were approached to sell their home with a promise of an allocation of a modern flat; however, most elderly men refused the offer. During a cycle ride one morning, Rahul had encountered a familiar face who excitedly informed the doctor that he had set up a small pharmacy in the village with the help of the *panchayat* leader. Rahul was surprised and confused at the same time. The two men cycled to the medicine store, where the doctor was reluctantly greeted by Partha, and Rahul had noticed a bold, green and white sign on the front door 'private doctor available for consultation'.

Rahul never missed the opportunity to visit Mathal, and during a brief visit to the medicine man, Rahul was informed by sad Mathal that he was no longer consulted or frequented by the villagers, and the government hospital's need to the people had diminished over time, as private medical care had sprouted up in the village; Only people who could not afford private medical care visited the district hospital. Rahul and his wife had also discovered this change during their short visits. The new appointed District Doctor met with Rahul on a few occasions and commented on the changing times in the village which had quickly accepted the privatisation of medical care and the lack of interest of the younger generation to challenge this unwarranted intrusion in their life.

In the comfort of his home in Kaliput, Rahul would often arrange impromptu social gatherings with his friends from the city; they knew his passion for writing and often during lighter moments, the doctor would be cajoled by his friends to write about his experience and the changing life of Panchkuri where he served as a community doctor. Rahul had given this idea a serious thought, and on a Sunday, he penned his first essay in the large notebook that Trisha had gifted him, with the aim of publishing it in the local newspaper. Rahul thought deep as he wrote about his life in a remote village and the fast changing landscape of the green land and the confusion the tribal people had to experience. The cultural and social changes in the village were all too apparent, and modern life had replaced the old traditions and practices of the older generation. The village was fully electrified and most houses boasted of a TV and other household luxuries. Slowly and steadily, most of the people had embraced modern life and the roar of the mountain lions was rarely heard. The thatched huts were replaced with bungalows. However, to his delight, Rahul was informed that the annual spring festival was still the highlight of the year and its popularity was well publicised in main newspapers. Although the economy of the land had improved marginally, farming was no longer a chosen profession for the villagers, as young men preferred the office jobs and setting up their own business. As Rahul had gathered the most significant achievement for Panchkuri was the primary school and its important contribution to children's education. The memories of struggle and victory were attributed to the champions of the cause, despite the political pressure and manipulation from the political parties in the big city. The river journey was quicker as steamboats had replaced the *nouko* (county boats) and riverbanks were lined with small shops. Rahul did not miss the scenes of brisk business on both sides of the river.

In the meantime, the elusive deputy *panchayat* leader, Konso, had secured a lucrative job in the city and very few people were unaware of his shrewd role in antagonising some of the activists to boycott the school in the village. However, soon the senior members had been informed about his devious intention, and within a short time, the leader had very few people who he could call friends. He had been totally alienated. But his crafty disposition was a blessing to a favoured political party as he made many friends and climbed up the corporate hierarchy in the city.

For the urban population, Panchkuri had become a tourist hotspot and many small bazars had been set up to meet the demands of urban visitors. For many of the simple villagers, the change was both confusing and rapid, as they struggled to accept the transformation of their beautiful village, and the dissemination of its traditions and practices was a heavy price to pay. The first primary school of the village was a timely blessing, and Rahul and Trisha often paid a visit to the school and met the teachers and children. To the young married couple, a familiar sight was to see and hear groups of elderly men sit in the portable tea stalls and reminisce about the past glory of Panchkuri and to the few octogenarians the sudden urbanisation of their land had astonished them, and the loss of the small hamlet's identity had saddened many people. The lush green fields were spotted with modern houses, and the thatched colourful huts were uprooted. During conversations, Rahul had discovered that the most affected person in the small village was Mathal as he had not anticipated the sudden changes in the land that he loved. The recognition as an experienced man of Ayurveda, Mathal's name had also slowly vanished, much to the disappointment of the newly married couple.

For most of the natives of Panchkuri, it was a story of a former blessed land and its forgotten people.

### The End

\*\*\*\*

CPSIA information can be obtained
at www.ICGtesting.com
Printed in the USA
BVHW051945011019
559918BV00015B/225/P